D0436270

WHAT
COMES
with the
DUST

WHAT
COMES
with the
DUST

· a novel ·

GHARBI M. MUSTAFA

Arcade Publishing • New York

First Edition

This is a work of fiction. Names, characters, places, and incidents are either the product of the author's imagination or used fictitiously.

Arcade Publishing books may be purchased in bulk at special discounts for sales promotion, corporate gifts, fund-raising, or educational purposes. Special editions can also be created to specifications. For details, contact the Special Sales Department, Arcade Publishing, 307 West 36th Street, 11th Floor, New York, NY 10018 or arcade@skyhorsepublishing.com.

Arcade Publishing® is a registered trademark of Skyhorse Publishing, Inc.®, a Delaware corporation.

Visit our website at www.arcadepub.com.

10 9 8 7 6 5 4 3 2 1

Library of Congress Cataloging-in-Publication Data

Names: Mustafa, Gharbi M., 1967– author.
Title: What comes with the dust: a novel/Gharbi M. Mustafa.
Description: First Arcade edition. | New York: Arcade Publishing, 2018.
Identifiers: LCCN 2018000587 (print) | LCCN 2018005915 (ebook) | ISBN 9781628729498 (ebook) | ISBN 9781628729474 (hardcover: alk. paper)
Subjects: LCSH: Yezidis—Iraq—Crimes against—Fiction. | IS (Organization)—Fiction.
Classification: LCC PR9170.I73 (ebook) | LCC PR9170.I73 M87 2018 (print) | DDC 823/.92—dc23
LC record available at https://lccn.loc.gov/2018000587

Cover design by Erin Seaward-Hiatt
Cover photographs: iStockphoto

Printed in the United States of America

What comes with the dust goes with the wind.

WHAT
COMES
with the
DUST

Prologue

and an Ancient Yazidi Prophecy

WHEN THE Supreme God created Ta'us Malik, the Head of the Angels, from His illumination, He instructed him not to bow to other beings. God then created the other archangels, ordered them to bring Him Akh—dust—from Ard—the Earth. From this Akh, He built Adam. God blew life into Adam with His breath and instructed the archangels to bow to His new creation.

All the archangels obeyed except for Ta'us Malik. "How can I submit to another being? I am from Your illumination while Adam is made of dust."

Ta'us Malik wept for seven thousand years, and his tears of remorse filled the Seven Sacred Jars, thus quenching the fires of Hell. The Supreme God then entrusted the world to the care of the Seven Archangels led by Ta'us Malik.

He revealed himself as a rainbow halo around the sun and then descended to Earth in the form of a magnificent peacock to endow the world with beauty and abundance.

He landed in *Lalish* canyon, the heartland of northern Mesopotamia, among the Yazidis, the first people, who had inhabited the Garden of Eden. From these blessings, Ta'us Malik, the Peacock Angel, became a central figure in the religion of the Yazidis, a religion that combines elements from the ancient Mesopotamian and Persian religions as well as Judaism, Christianity, and Sufi-Islam.

The misconception of identifying Ta'us Malik with the figure of Satan in Judeo-Christian faiths and Iblis in Islam has led to a long history of persecution of the Yazidis as Devil worshipers.

An Ancient Yazidi Prophecy

When Qappia Asmani, the Gate of Heaven, makes its appearance in the sky, the Fifth Age of this world will commence, beginning the era of purification of humankind on Earth. Ta'us Malik, the Peacock Angel, will instruct the holy men around the world, who will in turn deliver the message to the representatives of all nations.

This Fifth Age will begin in a time of war that will be waged against not only the Yazidis but all of humanity. Thousands of shrieking black crows will swarm across the deserts, and rivers of innocent blood will flow. This war will force the Yazidis to abandon their homes and migrate to the four corners of the Earth.

During this Great War, the Yazidis will be a source of enlightenment to the Muslim and Christian nations. The Lalish Temple and other ancient holy shrines will be safe havens for the displaced people who seek shelter.

The war will be a war of ideals, pitting the spiritual against the material. The spiritual message will prevail and will be carried forward by those who survive to create a new world. This new Golden Age will be ushered in by Ta'us Malik.

TODAY IS Nazo Heydo's wedding day, and today she will set herself on fire. Wearing her white gown, Nazo walks toward the bathroom door. In her right hand, she clutches the handle of a kerosene jerry can. Once inside, she turns and locks the door. A cold wind whistles through the broken panes of the small window. Her body shivers as she leans against the blue tile of the wall. She removes her veil and throws it on the floor. Warm tears streak her cheeks as she raises the heavy jerry can over her head. In shallow breaths, the odor of the kerosene fills her nostrils with the fumes of despair and anguish. She pours it over herself until she is soaked in it. The kerosene washes away the layers of her caked-on makeup, leaving her face pale and sheer.

Outside the room, she hears the chanting voices of men celebrating with the groom. She pulls the matchbox from her left-hand bridal glove. Then, she closes her eyes for a moment and listens to her heartbeat drumming in her ears.

With focused determination, she strikes the matchstick against the box. She opens her eyes and watches the yellow flame surge upward. As she brings the flame close to her face, memories trickle through her head, only to fall away with the kerosene and the beads of sweat dropping onto her gown.

Her mind drifts to that blazing August afternoon five months ago, when she walked into the courtyard of her family's farmhouse on the northern outskirts of the village. Fresh white paint streaked the old mudbrick wall as Qasim, Nazo's older brother, pressed the tip of the paintbrush against it. He had to hurry and finish painting the house walls before the new furniture arrived from Dohuk tomorrow afternoon.

Nazo wrinkled her nose at the odor of the fresh paint coming from the open windows of Qasim's room. She picked up her bucket and walked toward the main gate with the intention of fetching water from the nearby well. A shortage of water plagued her family in the summer months.

"*Daiky*, we're out of water again," shouted Nazo.

Her mother crouched on the thick mud layer of the flat roof, drying black figs in a massive plate. "That's odd. The reservoir was full this morning. Must be that donkey again." Eyeing the white donkey fastened to the huge mulberry tree that shaded the courtyard, she added, "I still cannot understand how a donkey learned to open the tap with his teeth. What a careless donkey! If he can learn how to open it when he's thirsty, he should learn how to close it when he's done."

Nazo could hardly suppress a mischievous giggle as she walked out through the main gate. There had indeed been enough water to meet the needs of an entire army unit. The poor donkey took the blame, but it was Nazo who had opened the reservoir tap this time. For reasons of her own, she longed to fetch more water from the Bira Zeytona well.

The windblown dust of the Arabian Desert fell like a blood rain from the sky of the Shingal region. The sun struggled to break through, but the cloak of dust choked its golden beams to a pale red all across the horizon.

Moments later, a cloud of dust splattered into the house and red dirt shrouded the freshly painted walls. By midafternoon the village had become a ghost town. Everyone took a siesta to escape the August heat. Swinging the handle of her bucket, Nazo hummed a Kurdish folk song as she walked up the rocky dirt track.

By the well, Nazo sat on the swing in the shade of the big fig tree. She leaned back and pushed off with her feet. Thoughts whirled in her head, and her heart raced faster than the swing. Tomorrow, she and Azad would meet before dawn in the backyard of her house. They would carry what they could fit in their shoulder bags and run toward the next village. There, they'd blend in, find a waiting car, and set off for the Turkish border. Then Azad's smuggler friend would help them cross the border on foot. In Turkey, he would drive them to Izmir. After that, they would board a dinghy and cross the Aegean Sea to seek asylum in Germany.

She and Azad had to blow their dreams into the universe like feathers in a whirlwind and wait for what Fate would return—a new land and a new life, unless it had something else in store for them.

She desperately wanted to leave the village and never look back. Her parents had arranged her engagement to her first cousin, Chato, a hotel manager from Baghdad, a few weeks before she had met Azad. With one leg a little shorter than the other, Nazo walked with a slight limp. She was born with developmental dysplasia of the hip, a genetic disorder attributed to Nazo's parents being first cousins. Sarah, her eleven-year-old sister, was born deaf and mute. Part of her wanted to be the dutiful daughter and marry her cousin. But with every limping step, she thought about the deformed children that she would bring into the world from this marriage.

Before she had met Azad, her life felt shallow, like swimming in her family's mud-hole pond where she could go through the motions but never reach anywhere. In Azad's eyes, she discovered the blue ocean. In his heart, she found a life ring.

Azad was not any young man! For Nazo, he was a sweet apple from the forbidden tree, and she had fallen for him literally the first moment their eyes had met at the village school. While trying to break her fall, Nazo had dropped the peacock-blue porcelain vase, a gift for her father, the headmaster. His fiftieth birthday present shattered on the cement steps, and the peacock feathers it had held drifted down the stairs.

A few drops of blood fell from her left index finger. Azad, the new substitute teacher, crouched down and squeezed her finger to compress her wound. Nazo gazed into his deep blue eyes and wished her blood would drip for eternity, so he would stay with her forever. He helped her to her feet, but Nazo's eighteen-year-old heart remained lying on the ground.

From that day on, delivering her father's lunch became Nazo's sacred mission. Around noon every school day, swinging the food basket with one hand, she walked to the school on the other side of the village. After delivering the meal to her father, she would seek out Azad. At first, she'd approach as if she were a frightened deer, but soon his bold ideas became the fabric of her dreams.

* * *

As Nazo kicked the swing higher, the scent of Azad's cologne filled her nostrils. Without a word, he slipped up behind her and guided the swing to a stop. Nazo leaned back to face him, her legs still pumping the air. He reached up for her green floral headscarf and pulled it off.

She giggled. "What are you doing?"

He flipped her headscarf and blindfolded her. Her laughter felt silent. All her senses burned, on alert for his next move. She felt the press of his thumb across her lips. Soft hands cupped her face and softer lips kissed her closed mouth. Her brow moistened from the heat of the forbidden kiss.

She broke free from him and yanked off the blindfold. With the exuberance of youth, she ran in a circle around the tree, teasing him. As the tips of her toes lifted off the ground, she danced to the beat of her heart drumming in her chest.

He lunged toward her and grabbed her around the waist. This time, they both fell, tumbling behind the wall that surrounded the well. Azad paused and undressed her with his eyes before he carefully flipped her hem up. He had touched her soul long before he swept his fingertips across her stomach.

Panting, he pinned her hands to the dusty ground. She had no power to swim against the tide of emotions that swept over her. She let herself drown under his touch. Their breaths mingled as he kissed her parted lips. The melody of her pleasure whirled on her tongue as their bodies danced together. His lips sparked an earthquake inside her, and she clung to him. Lost in new sensations, she dug her nails into his shoulder blades as he pressed himself into her for the first time.

She burned in his soft flames and melted in the warmth of his body heat. The scene around her shifted under a pink-tinted sky. Butterfly wings fluttered across the sunbeams as if they stirred the breeze. His breath tickled her neck as he collapsed on her body. Then he lay beside her.

Deeply in love, Nazo did not give herself in small pieces. She gave down to the marrow of her bones. She threw her arms around his neck and squeezed him tight. Though a smile crept up inside her, her lower lip quivered, and hot tears raced from the corner of her eyes. She wondered why making sweet love should bring such bitter tears.

He touched her cheek to wipe the tears from her face with the tips of his fingers.

"Azad," she breathed softly, "life is beautiful when we open our eyes and see its true colors."

"Colors?" He sighed. "Life here is like sitting inside four walls and watching the world on an old black-and-white TV."

Her elopement tomorrow would bring disgrace and pain to her family, and the thought became a crushing weight on her chest. "Can't we bring colors into our lives here?"

A cluster of black crows swooped over their heads and nestled in the tree, sending dust into the air.

"Clouds of dust conceal the rainbow of colors in the sky here. Perhaps we could change the color of our eyes, but the world we see would be the same."

"Never change the color of your eyes—I see all the colors of the world through them."

"There are so many blue-eyed men in Germany. I can't believe mine will be special anymore."

Nazo brought her face so close to his that the tips of their noses touched. She whispered, "You wouldn't say that if you could see your own eyes."

They kissed one more time, then he rose and slapped the dust from his pants.

"Don't go!" Nazo leaned toward him, hoping that another kiss might hold him with her just a moment longer.

"I must." He cracked his knuckles—something he always did when he was nervous. "The Daesh keep drawing nearer to our villages. I have to check on our arrangements. By sunset tomorrow, we will breathe in a safer land."

"But you are my safe land." Nazo pulled him close.

He squeezed her hands. "Tomorrow at dawn, in the backyard of your house, I'll howl like a wolf; that will be the signal."

"Oh, my cute wolf, I'll follow you anywhere you want me to go. With you, every corner of this world will be my Heaven."

He kissed her one last time. Then, through tears not yet shed, she watched him go.

Glancing around, fearful someone might have seen them, Nazo climbed to her feet. Like beating a Persian rug, she slapped the dust from her pale cream dress. She fixed her head-scarf, then plopped onto the swing. Azad owned her soul, and now he had become a part of her flesh. Tomorrow morning, would he look at her the same way as before? Would her heart survive if he failed to come tomorrow?

Azad was born to be different from the other young men in the village. As a new teacher assigned to the school from another town, Azad never tried to fit in with the village community. This intimidated the people around him, and most villagers didn't know how to deal with him. They thought of him as a snobbish town boy who ridiculed the prevailing social habits and beliefs. The villagers were not used to a person who strayed outside the flock and stepped into their taboos. They tried to alienate him and make him feel odd, yet Nazo was swept away by his eccentric ideas and his desire to create a different path in life.

Nazo leaned over the low concrete wall and filled her bucket. She gazed at the water in the bucket; instead of her reflection, the falling face of her mother stared at her. She shook the bucket, and the image shifted to her little sister Sarah. With a sullen face, she stood crumpling her lips with her fingers. Shaking off their expected disappointment in her, Nazo hefted the bucket onto her left shoulder and headed back to her house. As she walked, tiny streams of water splashed out of the bucket and soaked her curly hair. The back of her neck tickled as the fresh water dripped down onto her shoulders. A cloud of dust lifted off the ground and stretched out toward the horizon. The specks of dust landed on her hair and formed tiny clumps of mud.

Today she had made her first step between Heaven and Hell. She'd stepped onto the forbidden path. Her feet sank into the quicksand of illicit pleasure, and her soul fell into the claws of guilt. Yes, she had lost her virginity, her badge of honor, but did she still have her purity? Nazo wondered.

She prayed in her heart to Khuda Mazin, the Supreme God, and Ta'us Malik, the Peacock Angel, to grace her with forgiveness, for she knew she had committed an eternal sin.

When she arrived home, she emptied the bucket into the small metal reservoir behind the gate. Sarah ran to Nazo, making her strange noises and flipping her hand in the air against Nazo's face. The gesture meant she was asking about Nazo's rendezvous. Nazo threw her arms around Sarah and kissed her forehead. Then, taking her sister aside, Nazo flashed some hand gestures that made Sarah put her hand over her mouth.

Nazo acted as Sarah's ears and tongue to the passing world. They conversed in a sign language of their own that no one else in the world understood. Their mother, burdened with housework and farming, had assigned Sarah as Nazo's responsibility ever since she was a little baby. They were like one soul dwelling in two bodies. With no close female friends, Sarah became her box of secrets. The only thing Nazo could never gesture to her was tomorrow's elopement.

Once Nazo was in the rear room, her mother called to her and motioned for her to sit down. Nazo leaned her back against the wooden cupboard door, and her hand squeezed the edge of the foam mattress. She stared blankly at the erratic array of pictures on the wall. Then she fixed her gaze on the silk hand-embroidered picture of the holy Peacock Angel. She yearned for a spiritual renewal. Like the peacock, she needed to shed her feathers in order to regenerate ones more brilliant than before.

Mother slipped her left hand into the mustard-yellow waist-band that wrapped around her long white gown and pulled out something from the inner pocket. She unfolded her cracked fingers and revealed a pair of blue earrings resting in her palm. "Nazo, I bought these from a passing fortune teller yesterday to protect you from the Evil Eye."

She put the first earring onto Nazo's left ear and whispered, "Remember, other men are forbidden for you to wed. Never forget you are engaged to your first cousin. One day you will marry him and move into his house." She fastened the other earring on Nazo's right ear and whispered once more, "This is to serve as a reminder for you to always behave as you were brought up under my instruction. Remember, a decent girl will only lose her virginity to her husband on her wedding night. If she never marries, then a decent girl will die a virgin."

She gazed up at her mother's tattoo that started between the breasts and climbed upward like a vine toward her chin; the Tree of Life, which in ancient times was believed to have reached the sky, served as a symbol of immortality.

Nazo's eyes moistened, then she lowered her head in silence. Her lips did not respond to the call of her inner voice, which whispered, "Mother, what you are afraid of has just happened." She tried to speak but could only tremble.

As her mother's hand clasped her own, the sound of gun-fire broke the silence. Mother turned to the door. "Is there a wedding today? Poor bride. Who would marry on such a dusty day?"

Something inside urged Nazo to shout, "*Daiky*, today is my wedding!" but another short burst of gunfire stopped her.

As Azad strolled back to the school, happiness coursed through him. He had stolen Nazo's heart and now received her virginity. After their beautiful encounter, he craved an afternoon nap. As he trudged in silence, his face clouded. Sweat ran down his body as he thought of all the risks that lay ahead of them. Two things worried him the most: being caught by his fellow villagers eloping with an engaged girl, and crossing the Aegean Sea aboard a small boat.

Even as a child, he had feared the water, a fear his grandpa had never understood. Azad, a grandson of the famous fisherman Hassan Seydo, could not set foot in the lake. Whether in nightmares or waking visions, dead spirits called to him from under the waves. Every sunset of his youth, Azad had faced the sun and prayed that, after death, his soul would reincarnate into any form except a fish.

The other fishermen's children mocked Azad, calling him the blue cat because he screamed in panic each time Grandpa dragged him onto the boat to teach him to fish. Desperate, Grandpa took Azad by the hand and walked to the Sheikh's house. The Sheikh moistened the *dazzi*, a piece of thread, with his tongue and mumbled a prayer. Then he tied it tight around Azad's neck to protect the boy from his panic attacks. In a few days, the *dazzi* silenced the voices coming from under the waves, but Azad's aquaphobia persisted.

The day came when Grandpa realized the futility of his efforts. Seeing the agony on the child's face the instant the white boat came into sight, Grandpa loosened his grip on Azad's neck. "You worthless kid. Go to school then. May the chalk dust fill your eyes forever. Be a wage slave and compete with the others all your life to survive."

Grandpa had never liked school. He thought people could learn more from a fish than from another human. But as the years passed, his curse turned into a prophecy, and Azad became a schoolteacher.

A few months ago, Azad had packed his luggage and bid his grandpa goodbye to travel to the Shingal region for his first teaching assignment.

Grandpa's face looked scrunched as if he had spent the night tossing and turning. He placed a kiss on Azad's head. A single tear ran down his cheek and disappeared into his snow-white beard. He tore the *dazzi* from Azad's neck and left for his boat.

After Azad's parents had died under mysterious circumstances when he was three, Grandpa had raised him as his own child. Azad had no memory of his parents and grew up thinking Grandpa was his father. He often asked Grandpa about his mother, but every time he asked, the subject abruptly changed to the weather for the next day's fishing.

Not until he was seven, when Grandpa took him for school registration, did Azad hear the middle name attached to his, Murad, a name he had never heard before.

The next day, Grandpa helped Azad get into his school uniform, a white shirt and gray pants. Azad couldn't wait to join other kids at school.

Grandpa dipped the wooden comb into a cup of warm water and slicked back Azad's blond hair. "Azad, my son, this is your big day. I want to tell you something before you hear it from someone else. Murad, my deceased son, is your biological father." He released a deep sigh as if a huge load had been lifted from his chest.

Before Azad could move his lips to ask his first question, Grandpa continued: "Both your parents died in a boat accident when you were a little child. We reached the capsized boat that day, but we could never retrieve their bodies from the lake."

As Grandpa fixed the schoolbag on his shoulders, Azad turned and put his arms around Grandpa's left leg, then burst into tears.

Grandpa patted his head. "Go, boy. You don't want to miss your first class."

Azad wiped his tears with his sleeve and walked to the door. "Goodbye, Dad."

* * *

17

Now Azad planned to stray even further from his grandpa. Remaining in the village would mean, at best, a life in chains for him and Nazo. He must tame his fear of water in order to make their trip to Europe. He hoped, with Nazo on board with him, all his fears would evaporate like seawater in the heat of the sun.

Neither water nor dust would destroy his dream of a free life with Nazo at his side. No matter how well fed, a caged bird would always keep its eyes on the blue sky. He might have been born caged by the words of other humans, but inside he remained wild and free. His wings had grown strong enough to carry Nazo and him far from here.

He refused to sacrifice his soul on the altar of conformity. For him, life was not about what he was supposed to do. It was about doing what he loved.

If he stayed and conformed into a version of himself that would be acceptable, he would lose the only thing he valued in this place—Nazo. No matter how much love he poured into her, Nazo could not wed Azad. For their love to blossom, they must break free from their people and travel to the farthest lands in search of a place to build their home.

One evening when he had expressed reluctance to elope with Nazo, Grandpa gave him a weary look. He downed his second narrow glass of ouzo and wiped his thick, bushy mustache with the back of his hand. "Azad, you can't be afraid to go fishing because your ass might get soaked." He'd put his cracked hand on his grandson's shoulder and continued, "Never expect narcissus to bloom in a desert. Go, son. Seek new shores. Let the storm in your soul stir your blood and rip the roof off your sane mind. To be normal is to be sick. I've never met a rational man who was genuinely happy. Dare to be crazy if you want to enjoy life to the fullest."

Azad rubbed his sweaty hands through his hair. "Dad, the image of angry villagers with small rocks in their hands encircling me and Nazo has never left my mind."

Grandpa's grin had grown wide on his tanned and wrinkled face. "Excuses are the shields of the cowards. We are voyagers in a sinking boat. If you want something so badly, you must make it happen. The love in your heart ought to silence the voices in your mind. Go ahead. If love compels you to cross the Aegean, then bury your fears beneath its waters. Only the excuses confuse our lives, not the reality."

* * *

Startled by the sound of gunfire, Azad dropped to the ground a few yards before he reached his residence at the school. A classroom window on the second floor burst into shards. As he cautiously stood, a cloud of dust swirled around him, kicked up by two speeding Humvees that encircled him. Azad froze in place while an ISIS man with a laptop and two other fighters jumped from the Humvees and approached.

One of the fighters kicked Azad in his chest, making him fall to the ground. "We are the men of the Islamic State. Confess your full name."

"Azad Murad Seydo." With the name, the image of a capsized boat drifting along in the current floated on his consciousness. Once again, the voices of the dead spirits called him from under the waters.

The man browsed through his laptop for a moment, then raised his head. "The school's English teacher?" He grinned with shark's teeth. "You might be of some help to us."

One of the fighters spat on Azad's face. "Blue eyes and blond beard! Your mother must have slept with a European man behind your father's back."

"These sons of Satan; they carry Aryan genes," said the man with the laptop. Then he turned to the second fighter. "Yazidis never marry outsiders to retain their pure bloodline."

The second fighter thought for a moment, then raised his eyebrows as if he'd come up with a brilliant idea. "We ought to impregnate their women to cleanse this Aryan bloodline!"

"God bless, that would be a sacred mission!" the man with the laptop said before turning to Azad. "The village is surrounded. Stay in the school building. You have three days to convert to our religion. If you don't profess your faith by reciting the Shahadah, if you don't do exactly as I say, I will delight in pulling out both of your blue eyes and feeding them to the crows."

OMED WAS known in the village as the Frowning Face because no one had ever heard his laughter or seen his smile. Omed followed Nazo every time she fetched water from the well or went to the melon farm. He woke up early that morning and wrote a love letter to her. He slid the letter into the left pocket of his new long-sleeve pink shirt.

On the road to the Bira Zaytona well, Omed sat on a small rock among the olive trees and waited for Nazo to pass. While he swung his legs to focus on his shattered thoughts, he remembered his last encounter with Nazo.

One afternoon two weeks ago, Nazo had walked home with a big basket of melons on her head. Omed was walking a safe distance behind her when one of the melons fell from her basket unnoticed. He gathered his courage and hurried toward her.

"Hey, girl, one of your melons fell off."

Nazo stopped and turned to face him. "What do you want from me?"

"Your melon." Omed kneeled down to pick up the cracked melon from the ground.

"Oh, never mind," she replied.

"No"—he stared at her large breasts for a moment—"let me hold your melons."

"What?" snorted Nazo.

Omed couldn't hold back his smile. "I mean the melons on your head."

Nazo's face flashed with heat. "No, thanks." She looked to the dented melon in his hands. "Keep it for your dinner, or feed it to your donkey at home."

"I don't have a donkey at home."

"Strange, every family has at least one donkey."

Omed mustered the best smile he could, while he held the smashed melon close to his heart.

"You know, you have a cute smile," said Nazo.

Hearing that, Omed had walked away without a sense of direction. What she couldn't know was that Omed only smiled when he saw her. The yellow juice from the melon dripped from his hands onto his pink shirt. His nostrils fluttered wildly as he sniffed its aroma. He was light on his feet, floating on a cloud. Back home, Omed had chewed on the small dried chunks of that melon for days, and kept the seeds in a small plastic bag to plant them in his backyard next growing season.

Now, he gathered his thoughts as he walked toward the fig tree where Nazo swung in the distance. He froze in place, and his numb fingers released the letter he'd written to her as he watched Azad approach her and kiss her neck. Omed picked up his letter from the dusty ground.

Why won't you fall for me? My hands are strong enough to hold you.

I find you in everything I see or do, yet you see everything around except me.

I might not be good looking, but I will make you look more beautiful.

I promise to always be who I am—not some fake copy of Mr. Perfect.

I might not be funny, but I will not stop until I make you laugh.

I might struggle in school, but I am ready to learn everything about you.

I might look cold, but I promise we will both burn together in my fire.

I want to enjoy your fragrance, but I'm also ready to bleed from your thorns.

I might have nothing to give you now, but I have hands willing to blister to make you a home.

I am not some smooth talker who will play with your head to get you to bed.

Illusions are not my game. True love is my aim.

Mr. Nice might send you roses; I want to plant melons for you.

I might feel weak and insecure, but my arms will be your safe haven.

Fall for me—I will never break your heart as mine already is.

Fall for me—because together we will rise.

No one was immune to love, the most ancient virus in human history. It filled Omed's blood before he even knew it, eating up his body and soul. Today had started with such promise, yet anguish now shadowed his eyes and hollowed his face. He watched from a distance as Nazo and Azad made love behind the water well.

Then he scurried back home. He pulled out the key from a crack in the mud wall beneath the boarded window. The rusty metal door scraped in rhythm with the scoring on his soul.

He walked straight into his bathroom and shut the door. Sitting on the floor, he unfolded the crumpled letter in his hands. With his love dying, he screamed it out, seeing no sense in pretending he wasn't hurt. He pulled a razor blade out of his cabinet to paint another picture, to tell the story of how he had fought for love and lost. The razor served as his brush, and his canvas this time was his chest.

Omed's mother had died when he was eight years old, but he had weathered that loss by punching other children. He inflicted pain on others hoping he would feel better, but instead it heightened his feelings of anger, guilt, and frustration.

As he grew older, he realized that hurting himself was far more cathartic than hurting others. This epiphany began with a rash desire to punch walls and head-butt doors after he'd lost all his remaining family—his father and his two sisters—to a suicide bomber who'd targeted his village a few years back. For six months after that tragedy, he'd let his beard grow. When he shaved it, he discovered the art of cutting. Ever since, cutting became his only true friend, and his razor became his caring enemy. While he may have started with a few superficial cuts, they soon grew deeper, and he cut more frequently, up to seven times per day.

He wore long sleeves in the heat of the summer to cover his carvings from the villagers. With that outfit came the mask of a powerful man. He lived in a society where crying was strictly the business of children and women. He had to wear his frowning face every day while, beneath his clothes, his body stung and bled like his heart. His favorite place to do the cutting was the bathroom, and his favorite time was night, when he could lay aside his tough mask and be himself.

Nazo had been his hope for a new family. He could've stopped cutting for her. He had imagined Nazo to be his canvas and his gentle, loving hands to be the brush—her sacred body, his temple for the most elegant portrait that he craved to paint. Many nights in his dreams, he poured all his colors on her and with each color came a shiver. He had flown high, where nothing existed except Nazo and him.

Yet all his hopes died today. All his life he had dreamed of flying. Now his dream flew away instead and left him once more prey to the claws of loneliness. Now he had to fly the only way he knew how. Physical pain would be his wings to carry him to a world where the notion of pain did not exist.

Not only were beautiful things painful, but painful things were also beautiful. He'd learned that pain was a personal privilege. Pain was the only thing he had control over in his life now. But he still wondered if one pain could erase another.

The physical wounds healed with some scars, but the cuts in his soul were so deep he feared them permanent. The only thing that could equal the pain inside him was the relief of feeling the physical pain on his skin. Nothing in everyday life could make him feel the way cutting had made him feel. It was his secret world of blood, pain, and pleasure.

While his close friends looked at his cuts with disdain, he saw beauty in each line. He counted twenty-four small cuts on his hands, legs, and chest. A few days back, he had used a broken piece of glass to engrave her name into his pale, skinny wrist. Cutting, he realized, couldn't bring Nazo into his life, but he wanted her to be a part of his flesh and blood.

The name of a perfect girl engraved into the body of a complete loser and a living disaster. Nazo overwhelmed his mind, but for her, Omed realized now, he was not even an option.

This time he had to cut deep to bring relief as the images of Nazo and Azad haunted him. Their giggling under the tree echoed like thunder in Omed's ears. When the blade sliced his torso open, he felt a sense of tranquility and holiness, like a follower of some mystic Sufi faith. He slid the razor over his skin and drew an X where his heart used to be. His blood stood out, stark red against his skin. His tears blended with his blood and created a new tableau. As he watched the trails of blood flowing down his chest, it allowed him to forget, for a few moments, the devastating image of his love and her lover. The pain over his heart lessened the pain inside his heart.

He burst into laughter, then let out a piercing cry. He couldn't tell if it was a cry of ecstasy or a plea for help. After dipping his fingertip into his flowing blood, he stared at it, lost in thought. Then he rinsed away the blood and cleansed his cuts with an antiseptic. He took out his lighter and set fire to the letter he'd written this morning to Nazo. The smell of the burning paper filled his nose. He brought the flames closer, until they made contact with his chest and singed the huge X over his heart. The sting was intense, but it felt good.

Through his half-shattered mirror, he peered at his painting, two slices, almost three inches each. He wanted Nazo to see his X-ed-out heart and feel guilty. He hated what she'd done today but could never hate her. *Would Nazo believe me if I said to her, "I would easily die for you"?*

While he was immersed in his thoughts like a mountain in the clouds, death continued to whisper in his ears. A heavy knocking at the front door startled him. He slipped back into his shirt. As he darted out of the bathroom, he stumbled into three armed men clad in black Afghan-style baggy trousers and white turbans standing right in front of the bathroom door. One of them shoved a thick arm against Omed's throat and pushed him back inside. They pinned him to the bathroom wall.

Some of the cuts on his body remained visible, so one of the men ripped off Omed's shirt. "You're an infidel and a cutter," the man yelled. He reached for a huge knife attached to the belt on his right hip. He pressed the knife to Omed's throat. "Slicing is my profession. I'll give you a choice: your head or your penis."

The world waited in silence. Omed's throat tingled as the man began sliding the tip of his knife in a half circle around his neck. As if he had fallen into a deep slumber, Omed closed his eyes.

The man moved his knife down, across Omed's body, to his privates. "Decision time."

"I don't mind either one of them. Both are useless," Omed uttered calmly with his eyes still closed.

When the three men heard this, they burst into a gale of villainous laughter.

The second man, still laughing, put his hand on Omed's shoulder. "Listen, we'll spare your life if you convert to Islam. That would enlighten your head and make it useful. And we'll let you marry one of our sisters who recently converted to Islam. I guess that would give your penis a purpose. Think it over. We'll be back in a few days."

When they released him, Omed collapsed to the floor. He sat with his head between his legs as the men slammed the door behind them.

* * *

In the evening three days later, Omed climbed the wooden ladder behind his mudbrick house to sleep on the roof. In that time of the year, villagers customarily escaped the swarms of mosquitos that raided their houses during the summer months by enjoying the cool night wind coming from the desert. He crawled into bed and secured his mosquito net. Before he lay back on his blanket and closed his eyes, he tucked a fresh, single-edged razor blade safely between his cheek and his teeth so that, no matter what happened in the coming days, he wouldn't be separated from his trusted enemy.

The lunatic buzz of mosquitos and the croaking of the frogs filled his ears. He blinked his eyes as he watched the night sky. The moon faded away and the stars played. He fixed his gaze on a bright star that never appeared to change position as time passed. It was Qappia Asmani, the Gate of Heaven, the North Star of Ta'us Malik. As the desert night breeze ruffled the mosquito net and caressed Omed's face, he fell into a deep slumber.

In his summer's night dream, Omed walked the streets of a burning city. Glowing trails of smoke faded away, and a rainbow emerged in the distant sky. A large bird arose from the beams of rainbow light and flew above the ruins. A moment after the bird's shadow passed over him, Omed watched the same large bird burst into the flames all around him. Frozen in place, he gazed at the creature burning itself into ashes with a single clap of its wings. Then suddenly a young phoenix, with an eagle's head but a peacock's feathers, emerged from the ashes.

Radiant and shimmering, the grand bird spread its wings and flew toward Omed. The phoenix picked Omed up from the ground and threw him on its back. With a thunderous screech, they streaked into the sky. The phoenix flew to a faraway kingdom and landed in a green forest among a group of children with pale faces and black circles under their eyes. Omed winced in pain as he watched the phoenix dig its claw into his right wrist. A trickle of blood ran from his wrist in a crimson ribbon. The children opened their dry mouths and drank from Omed's dripping blood. The color then returned to the children's faces, and they ran across the field.

Once more, the phoenix hefted Omed onto its back and flew to an empty desert. This time they landed among a group of sickly women lying on iron beds. Once more, the phoenix dug its claw into Omed's wrist, this time the left. Omed walked among the women and leaned over them so his blood dripped into their open mouths. The women then rose from their beds and walked with their bloated bellies into the shifting sands.

When the sun rose, the first orange rays speared through a hole in the roof wall and lit the mosquito net. Wiping the sleep from his eyes and the sweat from his forehead, Omed crawled out from under the net. He then put on his shoes and descended the ladder. As he put his foot to the ground, the same three ISIS fighters yanked him back by his throat.

One of the men growled, "Have you thought about what we told you?"

Omed scrunched his face for a moment, as if in thought, then grinned. "I'm good."

A blow landed under Omed's eye. "Even you, useless dick, refuse to convert to Islam!" shouted another fighter.

They dragged Omed to a small house across from the village school, where they'd sequestered a group of aged Yazidi clergymen who had refused to abandon their faith. Once they were inside, he could smell the odor of old urine mingled with the sweat of the clergymen, rank from fear and the heat of the August day.

One of the fighters turned to Omed. "You should show respect to your elders."

Another fighter cocked his assault rifle and directed it toward the group of the clergymen. He turned to Omed. "Urinate on them now. Otherwise we'll shoot all of them dead."

The old men sat cross-legged and motionless with their heads down. The eldest clergyman, his face desperate, raised his head slightly and gave Omed a weary look from under his lashes.

Omed's hand trembled as he pulled out his privates from his trousers. He walked toward the eldest clergyman, then, still trembling, sprayed his warm urine over the cleric's head.

Rage boiled inside him. He fought a tremendous longing to slit the ISIS men's throats with the razor blade held in his mouth. Yet any wrong move from him would lead to the massacre of the clerics in the room. Instead, Omed lowered his head and remained silent.

The ISIS fighters burst into evil laughter as they watched Omed's urine dripping from the clergyman's long white beard onto his white gown stained with old yellow spots.

"He baptized you so you'll smell good in the presence of your Satan," sneered one of the ISIS fighters.

Then the fighters pulled out their privates from their baggy trousers as well. The odor of fresh urine filled the air as they walked around the room and urinated on the rest of the clergymen. This had been going on every morning since ISIS besieged their village a few days back. They pushed Omed across the road to the school building, and as they did he saw Barakat, the mayor of the village, pacing back and forth, smoking in the yard of his house.

Today was their last day to convert, and Omed knew Barakat had informed the ISIS regional emir, Abu Jihad—a nom de guerre meaning father of Jihad—that the villagers refused to convert to Islam. Supposedly, this would lead to no harm, Abu Jihad had assured him, but Barakat didn't look so certain.

Abu Jihad had declared that the villagers would be allowed to abandon their village safely after they willingly handed over all their cash and valuables. Then ISIS would transport them to Mount Shingal where they could join thousands of other Yazidi families from the nearby villages who had fled during the night. All the villagers were to gather in the two-story school building this morning on Abu Jihad's orders.

AT DAWN, Nazo sat at the tiny wooden window in her room. She waited in the darkness, her ears alert for Azad's howl from behind the house. As time passed, she squeezed harder on the edges of her shoulder bag on her lap.

The gray morning light crept into the room through the slightly parted blinds. She threw her bag under the bed and paced back and forth across the room. A scream built within her, but she let her tears fall in silence. She felt sick. Her stomach knotted with cramps of disappointment and guilt. She hurried to the bathroom and hung her head over the sink.

On her way back, she caught the smell of fresh brewing coffee scented with sweet cardamom. Her father was in the kitchen preparing his Arabic coffee before he left for school. She collapsed on her bed and surrendered to the storm of gloomy thoughts that burdened her mind.

After an hour, she rose and headed for the main door. She couldn't wait until noon to bring father his lunch at school. As she stepped outside the house, she glanced at a distant caravan of pickup trucks emerging from the dust. Black flags flapped wildly above the heads of armed men in black fatigues who were standing behind machine guns mounted in the beds of their trucks.

In one brisk move, Nazo turned back and ran into the house. "Daesh! Daesh are here!" Nazo screamed.

Her brother Qasim, who was sitting in front of the TV flipping through news channels with his back to the door, sprang up and ran over to the table to grab his shoes.

A knock sounded at the door followed by a voice shouting, "Islamic State. Open the door, or you'll lose your heads."

Nazo grabbed Sarah and ran into the rear room as their mother collapsed to the corridor floor, sucking the edge of her headscarf into her mouth to suppress her screams. Nazo watched through a crack in the door as Qassim turned toward the small iron door to the backyard, but a louder knock froze him in place.

"The house is surrounded. You have ten seconds to open the door, or grenades will fly."

As Qasim walked to the door, a spark of fear pierced Nazo's heart. With each heavy step he took, dark images came to her mind, each more terrible than the last.

Men clad in tracksuits, their faces covered with checkered Arabian headdresses, rushed through the main door. They pinned Qasim down on his belly and tied his hands behind his back.

A man with an open laptop kneeled down and grabbed him by his hair. Then he shoved Qasim's head inches from the laptop screen. "Qasim Heydo, isn't this a photo of you dressed as a Peshmerga? A Yazidi infidel and a Peshmerga fighter, that's a fast ticket to Hell."

Two other men burst into the rear room and gestured with their guns until the girls joined their mother in the hall. Nazo grabbed Sarah's hand as the men forced them to their knees.

As they dragged Qasim across the floor toward the door, their mother threw herself upon her son's chest and wailed. She slid down and clung to Qasim's ankles as if she would never let him go. A rifle butt slammed into her shoulder, and another blow landed against the side of her head, weakening her grasp so they could pull Qasim away. Her eyes rolled to the back of her head. Nazo could only hope her beloved mother had merely been knocked unconscious.

When Nazo screamed and both girls ran to their mother, the strong men standing behind them grabbed them by their hair and pushed them toward the front door.

Right before their eyes, the ISIS men dragged Qasim, like a dog on his back, to the front yard.

Once outside, the men stood the two girls opposite their brother, who was now on his knees. Qasim raised his humble head and looked Nazo in the eyes. Still staring in silence, his eyes were hard as diamonds but shone with a ray of guilt. They had not spoken to each other for a week, because Qasim had slapped her face when he'd learned she was seeing Azad.

Nazo shouted at the top of her voice, "Love you, brother!"

As one of the men came for Qasim, Sarah squeaked in panic and urine coursed down her legs in fear. It was as if the thousands of silent screams inside Sarah's head could not make their way out, so they were forced to exit as urine from between her legs instead.

Without another word, a man behind Qasim raised a pistol and shot him in the back of his head. He fell forward onto his face and lay motionless. Sarah froze in place while Nazo threw herself on her brother's corpse. She pulled his bleeding head into her lap and wailed.

As the men piled back into their vehicles, one shouted to the girls, "You have three days to convert to Islam or suffer death."

* * *

Three days later, holed up in her family's home, Nazo watched a storm of emotions swirl across Sarah's face as she touched her gold necklace. She had worked hard the previous summer in the melon fields to save money to buy such a necklace. It had the shape of the yellow sun with twenty-one rays representing the Light of God in the Yazidi faith. It dangled from her neck by a long golden chain.

Sarah waved her hand angrily and shook her head when her father asked her to give him the necklace. Nazo then approached her and made a swift vertical palm sign across Sarah's neck to indicate that, if she did not give him the necklace, ISIS would slaughter everyone in her family.

Sarah touched her necklace once more and nodded her head. She flipped a V-sign on Nazo's arm to ask if she could walk to the school building wearing her necklace for the last time.

Three days earlier, the family had buried their only son. Today, they began their journey into the unknown. Father carried a suitcase with money. Mother held a small box in her hand that contained her wedding jewelry. As she walked, she lamented her lost son, wishing he could be with them now.

Nazo had taped her mobile phone to her neck securely beneath her long hair. It had been a gift from Azad that introduced her to a tiny world of photos and words where they had shared their intimate moments, their tears, and their laughter.

With every step Nazo plodded toward the school, her face became paler, and her breath became shallower. Once more, the sludge of guilt lay heavy in her soul as she remembered her rendezvous under the fig tree. Azad had disappeared since. She paused and prayed for him but was torn between her wish that he had escaped before ISIS besieged the village and her wish to see him in that very moment.

Their family was the last to arrive at the school. Other villagers were already lined up at the school gate. Men and women held onto their belongings with one hand and their children with the other. Abu Jihad stood close to his white jeep, surrounded by heavily armed fighters who supervised the process. Outside the school gate, ISIS had placed three large boxes labeled CASH, GOLD, and MOBILE PHONES.

When their turn came, Nazo's father came forward and dropped his money bag into the box before he entered the school. Mother followed and mumbled a curse in Kurdish as she dropped her jewelry in the box. Sarah tugged on her necklace and moved it back and forth on its chain.

An ISIS man standing next to the box labeled GOLD hollered, "Hurry up! We'll close the Hell Gate soon," then ripped the necklace from her neck and threw it into the box.

"She's deaf and mute. She can't hear you," Nazo said in a choking voice.

"Yeah? And I'm blind," yelled the ISIS man, grabbing Sarah by the shoulder to push her toward the gate.

Nazo noticed Abu Jihad gazing at her with his devouring wolf eyes and pointing her out to one of his fighters. She rushed through the gate, hoping to disappear among the crowd inside the school. Once she was in, she wedged herself between two matronly women who sat at the corner of the inner schoolyard with their children huddled around them.

The woman at her left struggled to soothe her crying twin babies. Seeing the agony on the woman's face, Nazo lifted one of the babies from their mother's shoulder onto her own lap. She rocked the baby and hummed a soft, melodic lullaby that sprang both from the love in her heart and the sparking fears in her head.

She stopped singing when a large shadow flowed over the ground in front of her and darkened the sunlight. Once she lowered the scarf on her head to a position that half-covered her face, she resumed her song, "Sleep my baby, sleep. Weep, weep till you sleep."

"What a cute child!" said the man as he kneeled in close and caressed the baby's head.

Recognizing Azad's voice, for one crazy moment Nazo wanted to place the baby aside and throw herself into his arms like a stray fledgling bird landing safely in its nest. She knew, however, that the slightest display of emotion would make her stand out.

Before she could decide what to do next, Azad rubbed the baby's back, and his hand landed on Nazo's. With a quick motion, he slipped a silver wedding band onto her finger, unnoticed as he cooed at the crying baby.

Nazo placed her trembling hand on his and squeezed it behind the baby's back. Then she pulled back her scarf and raised her head. They gazed into each other's eyes. Time stood still and mute. Their souls spoke in a language only they could hear.

All of Nazo's fears and worries evaporated like a dust storm giving way to the first rain.

As Abu Jihad and his men emerged from the school gate, Azad instantly withdrew his hand but leaned in close to Nazo's face. "Announce that you're a married woman," he whispered.

Nazo's sobs blended with her smile as her gaze moved back and forth between the ring on her finger and Azad hurrying away. After Azad disappeared into the crowd, she lowered her headscarf once more and leaned her head over the baby.

While she resigned herself to her own world of thoughts, a whiny voice burst forth and startled her. "We have come to remove every one of you from the ensnarled world of Satan and bring you into the kingdom of Allah the Almighty. Unfortunately, you choose to stay in this darkness rather than embrace the light of Islam," said Abu Jihad.

Then he ordered all the females and children to proceed to the upper floor while men and boys had to remain on the ground floor. A crowd of approximately eighty males were separated from the rest of their families and subdivided indiscriminately into two smaller groups. The first group included the mayor and Nazo's father. Azad and Omed found themselves with the aged Yazidi clergymen in the second group.

The sound of trucks pulling up and stopping at the gate generated fear and anxiety among the villagers. Tension filled the air as the ISIS fighters herded the first group across the yard and through the gate. They pushed about forty of the men and boys into the back of the three Kia pickup trucks and drove them toward the old cemetery on the southern outskirts of the village.

* * *

A short while later, Omed could hear the distant, muffled sound of machine guns. He guessed that an hour had passed before the ISIS fighters returned to load the remaining Yazidi men and boys into the three trucks. They drove their captives to the northern part of the village in the direction of Mount Shingal, about nine hundred yards in front of the Bira Zaytona well where Omed's heart had broken. They forced Omed and the others to stand in two lines with their hands on their heads facing the big fig tree where he had seen his beloved swinging just a few days earlier.

Abu Jihad sat on that same swing and rested his assault rifle across his lap. "We are not bloodthirsty murderers. We are soldiers of Allah implementing His Almighty Will upon the infidels. We do not kill because we like killing—we kill God's enemies. This will open the gates of Heaven to us. There is no place for you infidels here in the lands of the Islamic State or in any place on Earth. The only place that can embrace you for eternity is Hell. There is no other side. All should be on the side of Allah the Almighty—but you chose to serve your Satan."

As if instinctively, every man in the group seemed to know he had arrived at the end of his journey. All the faces near Omed blanched to the color of death. Their hands shook uncontrollably behind their heads. Yet Omed grew serene in anticipation of the moment the bullets would puncture his body. He was ready to take fresh pain and dark memories to his grave, prepared to die. The last thing he wanted to see before he could reunite with his family was the blood gushing forth from his wounds.

Everything seemed idyllic for him except the view. The fig tree and the swing were the only things that agitated him in his last moments.

Two ISIS fighters using their mobile phones filmed the fates of their Yazidi captives. The other ISIS fighters formed a firing squad. One of the ISIS fighters chanted, "*Takbir.*" All the other ISIS fighters chanted back, "*Allah Akbar*," as they waved their black flags over their covered heads.

Abu Jihad leaned back and, with a strong thrust of his feet, pushed off. The swing moved up into the air with his toes pointed toward the faces of the standing villagers. He pumped a few more times until he got higher into the air, and then he jumped off the swing, landed, and paced to the right side of the group. He signaled to the firing squad who stood opposite the two lines of villagers. The fighters fired their assault rifles with great zeal, and the villagers crumpled to the ground in the first hail of bullets.

Omed's fast and loud last moments passed slowly in silence. The blood of the eighty-five-year-old Yazidi clergyman he'd urinated on earlier spurted onto Omed's face before the cleric collapsed and slumped down over him. The ISIS fighters once again rained bullets on the helpless men lying on the ground to finish off any who still breathed. When the deep rumbling of an aircraft was heard flying overhead, the bullets stopped.

* * *

Women and children packed the classrooms on the upper floor, waiting to reunite with the men and boys of their families. Nazo stood by the classroom window holding the baby in her arms. Over the screams and cries of women and their children, she heard the sound of truck doors slamming outside, followed by the chanting voices of ISIS men as they celebrated their victory over the villagers.

Nazo swallowed the lump in her throat and fumbled with the filthy classroom curtain. Hot rays of sunshine hit her face as she peered through the tiny crack in the curtain. Blinking out at the bright sunlight, she could see a group of men standing in a circle around the empty trucks clapping their hands while others fired their guns in the air.

She backed away from the window, her eyes transfixed upon the images of blue butterflies on the curtain. Under Nazo's gaze, they floated in the air across the room. *If those butterflies could burst forth and fly, why can't I spread my wings and be a part of this divine mystery? Could little wings carry my body to be with Azad on Mount Shingal tonight?*

A tiny flash of joy flickered through her as she remembered how Azad had pierced her soul with his double-edged sword. He had poured his love into her, but now she felt empty again. The soothing sound of Azad's voice echoed in her ears, calming the erratic beat of her heart and silencing the Hell in her soul.

Then a group of fighters appeared at the head of the steps. They herded a third of the women and children down to the schoolyard, including Nazo and her family.

"Why did we hear gunfire a while ago?" asked an elderly woman.

"We were shooting some dogs." The ISIS fighter laughed.

"Son, what about our men? Did you send them to Mount Shingal?"

"We sent them to a higher place," he sneered.

Downstairs they separated the young women and unmarried girls from children and old women. Their horrified screams grew louder as the fighters drove the two groups into separate trucks. Nazo's mother clutched her and Sarah tight to her bosom and pleaded for mercy, watching in horror as the other girls were yanked from their mothers and dragged by their hair toward the trucks.

The ISIS men tore Sarah and then Nazo from their mother's grasp and forced them over to the truck on the left.

Abu Jihad and his men stood near the back of that truck. Nazo's heart pounded in her chest as she was forced closer. Sarah was pushed first into the truck.

As Nazo mounted the truck and reached for her sister, a hand clamped on her elbow and pulled her back. Sarah tried to jump down, but an ISIS member standing at the rear of the truck grabbed her by the hair, forcing her to stay put.

As the truck pulled away, Nazo screamed for her sister and struggled to free herself from Abu Jihad's firm grip. Abu Jihad knocked her down and dragged her to his jeep. He settled her into the passenger side. The jeep roared away, but she shoved away from him, intent on tumbling from the vehicle.

He yanked her hair and forced her head into his lap. "If you make any more moves, I will cave your head in with the butt of my rifle," he snapped. His voice trembled. "You are my share of the gift that God has bestowed upon the mujahedeen, His Almighty Warriors, in the sacred war against the pagan world."

There Nazo remained until they arrived at his house in one of the neighboring Arab villages. The odor of cow manure filled Nazo's nostrils as he dragged her out of the jeep and pushed her through a mudbrick house into a bedroom. There he forced her to watch a video of ISIS men strangling a woman to death. He warned her that she would suffer the same fate if she disobeyed him or showed any resistance.

Nazo's lower lip quivered, and she buried her face in her hands as he ripped off her clothes. Once she was naked, he yanked her off her feet and threw her on the bed. He tied her limbs to the old rusty bed with coarse rope. She swallowed a sob and braced herself for the worst. Then he knelt down in the middle of the room and prayed to God. In his eyes, what he was about to do was an act of devotion, a sacred rite that would draw him closer to his God.

As he rose over her, Nazo froze like a frightened rabbit caught in the glare of headlights. He knelt down between her thighs and inserted his rigid manhood into her. Nazo's stomach clenched, and she fought back the urge to vomit. He cupped her face in both hands as he mashed his putrid mouth on hers. Then he shoved his garbage-smelling tongue into her mouth as he came inside her. As the sound of his fires waned, he rose, shuddering in disgust, and left without a word.

Moments later, an elder wife with a tattooed chin and a black headscarf appeared at the door, her right hand gripping a kitchen knife. Nazo struggled against her bonds until her breathing became a pant, as the woman approached the bed. She stood over Nazo's head and spat on her face. "You filthy Yazidi infidel. Get up and wash the mujahedeen's clothes," sneered the woman as she leaned to cut the ropes.

Alone an instant later, Nazo tugged on her torn clothes. She crept to the bathroom, feeling sick. Her attacker's foul smell clung to her body and coated her mouth. She ran her fingers over her teeth and tongue until finally she threw up. She bathed several times and kept washing her mouth, but his foul smell continued to pervade her senses.

Defeated and drained, she slumped onto the tile, bending forward until her forehead touched the floor. "O Khuda, Supreme God, blow the breath of life into me and grace me with a new soul," Nazo pleaded.

She longed to visit the Sacred Lalish Temple, the spiritual heart of the Yazidis, and dip her fingertips in the holy waters of the Zam Zam that sprang from a cave inside. Bathing in water from the Zam Zam would purify her soul and wipe the foul smell from her body. She craved to stand in front of the pillars representing the Seven Archangels watching over humanity, led by Ta'us Malik, and tie her colored silk in a knot. Then she would make her only wish: to see Azad again.

She remembered her visit last year to the temple in October. It was the seven-day autumn Festival of the Assembly. The twin conical domes loomed in the orange light of the early morning as Nazo and her mother walked up the asphalt road to the narrow valley. Once they arrived, they wedged themselves among the thousands of Yazidis clad in colorful costumes who packed the modest courtyard. Nazo burned in anticipation to listen to the music of the sacred instruments, the handheld *daf*, a frame drum, and a *shebab*, a flute.

The five *Qawwals*, devotional musicians, emerged from the massive wooden door—two of them played the *daf* while the others blew on their *shebab*. Nazo swung her head to the tunes and mumbled the sacred hymns together with the temple's clerics. Immersed in the ecstasy of the tunes, Nazo rose to join the hundreds of pilgrims who clasped their hands in a huge religious dance circle across the courtyard. Yet she crouched back down to the ground when she remembered the limp in her right leg.

Later, Nazo approached an old sheikh clad in a roughly woven black shirt topped by a white robe. Nazo knelt to kiss the sleeve of his black shirt and offered to help him light the sacred fire on the long lines of small pads of cotton wicks soaked in olive oil.

Once done, the old sheikh asked her to throw pebbles blindly at two holes representing Heaven and Hell. It would show her where her soul would land on Judgment Day. She lobbed her three tosses toward her preferred fate, yet she failed to land any pebbles in either hole.

"Miss, it seems your soul will float across the universe, then reincarnate back to Earth," the old sheikh had commented.

Now, leaning against the bathroom wall in Abu Jihad's house, Nazo released a sigh. She knew she had sinned. She knew death would not turn her into an angel. Death would not free her from her sins. Her soul would continue to reincarnate in different bodies until she achieved a certain level of purity. This world was the place for her if she wanted to grow into a better human being. Then she would be eligible to enter the realm of Heaven and exist there for eternity. But Nazo's biggest fear was that she would reincarnate into the body of a person from another religion and lose her own faith.

In the corner of the bathroom, she spotted the pile of long shirts and baggy pants. Resigned to her fate, she pulled out a plastic washing bowl and added soap. Then she sat on a small wooden step stool. At her touch, warm water ran from the tap. As she dipped a shirt into the water, her tears dripped like a soft rain and crushed the tiny detergent bubbles in the middle of the bowl.

If Ta'us Malik had wept for seven thousand years, and his tears filled up the sacred seven jars, quenching the fires of Hell, can my tears quench the Hell inside me?

While a shirt was soaking, she dried her hands and took the phone from her neck. She opened the water tap and dialed Azad's number. She knew he would not hand over his phone to the ISIS fighters. She needed to hear his voice more than anything else in the world. Each time she redialed the number, she heard the same recorded message: "The number you have dialed is not available or out of the coverage area." Each time, her fingers shook more, and her heart pounded harder in her chest.

Before any dark thoughts disturbed her mind, she remembered the network connection would be weak for Azad on Mount Shingal.

A couple of hours later, she climbed the stairs leading to the roof, her legs shaking under the heavy bowl of laundry she carried on her head. Out of breath, she lifted the bowl from her head and put it on the ground. The scent of fresh laundry wafted in the air as she hung the clothes in the sun.

Nazo heard footsteps mounting the staircase to the roof. When she turned around, she saw a tall, dark-skinned woman walking toward her. "Did you wash them well?" the woman yelled.

Nazo nodded in agreement.

The young woman examined the long line of drying clothes before she turned to Nazo. "Yeah, you must feel fresh after good sex. I can see some good energy was pumped into you."

She leaned into Nazo. "I am the second wife of Abu Jihad. That old bitch, his first wife, is thrilled you're here because Abu Jihad will sleep with you now instead of me. She thinks she has had her revenge, but I won't let her enjoy this for long." She brought her lips closer to Nazo's ear. "Listen, Abu Jihad is out on a fighting mission. I'll take you downstairs. Change into my niqab, and in fifteen minutes a driver will take you to Shingal Town where you can reunite with your family."

NAZO BEGGED the driver to drop her close to the foot of Mount Shingal. He asserted that the instructions from his lady were to take her to Shingal Technical Institute where they held all the captive Yazidi women and children. When they arrived, the driver was told that all the captives had been transferred to the town of Talafar, one hour farther.

Finally, Nazo stepped into the primary school building in Talafar. At a distance, Nazo spotted a form dashing toward her. Sarah threw her arms around Nazo's neck and kissed her. Delighted, Nazo swept her sister off her feet and carried her into the schoolyard, smiling as her joyful tears fell on Sarah's neck.

They took a seat on the floor with their backs to the wall. Nazo looked around but couldn't see any elderly women. She turned to Sarah and tapped her tooth to indicate their mother's gold tooth, then flipped her palm in the air to ask where she was.

Sarah shook her head.

Nazo turned to a woman sitting on the ground close by, holding a baby on her lap. "Is there a chance that my mother's here?"

The woman shook her head and added, "The Daesh keep the elderly women in a separate building in Talafar and use them as servants. They separated the boys over the age of three from their mothers and took them so our sons can learn about their Shari'a law."

The woman broke into sobs. "My family tried to run to Mount Shingal, but our car broke down on the road. Soon we were surrounded by Daesh fighters. They pulled us out of the car and shot my husband and my eldest boy. He was only thirteen. Once we were brought here, they took my other boy, Bahzad, who is ten. Now he's trapped in some special school, learning the religion of the Daesh and combat skills. At least Jwan is still with me." The woman tore a bite from a cookie bar and fed it to her little blond daughter. A cute girl, Nazo decided, with a blue-beaded necklace.

Just then, a folded slip of paper fluttered from the bar's wrapping. The woman's eyes widened. "It must be a letter from my son. Bahzad secreted away a few bars of biscuits and a pack of milk from his allotment at school and sent them to his little sister. I can't read; will you read it to me?"

Nazo took the piece of paper from the mother's hand and unfolded it:

Mother,
I miss you and Jojo. I hope she enjoys the milk and the biscuits.
They have whipped me with a rubber hose a couple of times for not

memorizing my homework, but other than that, I am fine. I am
excited that they will move us to the military training camp next.
For that, I thank them. They will train me so I can shoot them
later. I will avenge my dad and my brother.

They told us that we are pagans, that our religion is wrong,
that we worship the Devil instead of God. They told us that the
Daesh religion is peaceful. I will write my next letter to God and
ask him why he let this happen.

I love you. B

The woman's quiet sobs burst into gushing tears as Nazo
finished reading her son's letter. She turned her head and fed
the chunks of biscuit soaked in milk to the infant on her lap.

A rough-looking, dark-skinned Turkoman with a massive head appeared at the classroom door. He signaled for the
woman to follow him and said she was his gift. When she
refused to move from her place, he snatched her infant Jwan
from her lap, hefted the baby onto his shoulder, and hurried
toward the door.

The mother leaped to her feet and attacked the man like
a wolf. Yet a single, well-placed punch knocked her to her
knees, and the man continued to kick her belly, while the baby
screamed on his shoulder. Then the Turkoman took off his
large leather shoe and placed it over her baby's little head.

He yelled, "Come with me, or I'll smash your baby's head
with this. Get up now if you want your howling brat back. You
are my *sabiya* now, my slave, and if you give me any more grief,
I will stomp the life from your precious daughter of the great
Shaitan."

The woman, sobbing, got up and accepted her little girl from his grip. Then she followed him out in silence.

After a few hours, four ISIS men walked into the primary school building, holding a register. They ordered the women to stand in line. For each young woman and girl, they demanded to know her full name, age, home village, marital status, and a number of children.

Then Nazo's turn came. "I'm eighteen and married to Azad Murad Seydo. We have no children." When they moved to Sarah, Nazo continued, "This is my younger sister, Sarah, a deaf-mute. She's eleven years old." This time, thankfully, no one doubted her word.

They herded the young girls and women like cattle onto trucks and drove them southeast toward the city of Mosul. Sarah lay in the bed of the truck with her head on Nazo's thigh. While Sarah bit her nails to the quick, Nazo prickled with her sister's nervous energy. She rubbed Sarah's brow and thought about how to cheer her up. Sarah's weak point was money notes; she loved to collect money as these notes brought her the things she wanted.

When Nazo had turned eighteen in April of that year, their mother asked her to make her wedding pillows for her future home, a Yazidi tradition.

As Nazo sat to embroider the two pillows, Sarah jumped all over the room, more excited than Nazo, not because Nazo would one day marry but because the pillows would bring Sarah a fat ransom.

Traditionally, when a Yazidi groom's family came to take the bride from her house with her belongings, the bride's sister would steal the bride's pillows and hide them. The sister would not return them until the groom paid her ransom.

As the truck bounced down the bumpy road, Nazo slipped a ten-thousand Iraqi dinar note into Sarah's hand. She unfolded the note. For a long moment, she gazed at the front, with a photo of a long-bearded Arabian Islamic astrologer and physicist named Alhazen. For all the world, the man looked no different from the ISIS fighter who'd shot their brother. Nazo understood when Sarah tossed the dinar note into the wind.

It whirled around in the air for a moment before clinging to the face of the ISIS guard who stood on the rear bumper of the truck. He grabbed the note and waved it at another ISIS fighter. "God has not only graced us with Yazidi girls but showered us with money as well," he shouted with a chuckle.

They crossed the old bridge over the Tigris River, which splits Mosul into two parts. There, they parked in front of a large wedding hall called Galaxy. The accompanying ISIS fighters ordered them to leap from the truck. Nazo jumped first and stretched out her arms for her sister. Sarah never hesitated; she threw herself into her sister's arms. They walked hand-in-hand into the hall.

As they entered, they tripped over the legs of Yazidi women and girls who sat dejected on the floor. Nazo and Sarah wedged themselves through the crowd until they found a place to stretch their legs and sleep overnight.

The next morning, men ordered Nazo and Sarah, among the fifty girls and women nearest the door, into buses and drove them to another location within the city, a heavily guarded, three-story building in southern Mosul. The girls and women were led to the basement.

The ISIS group leader, a man clad in a white Afghani outfit, appeared at the door and addressed the crowd. "God Almighty has blessed you this day, a day to remember, the day you convert from *kuffer* to the true religion of God. We are here to light your path to eternal paradise. Satan deluded you, dragging you into his world of evil. Forget all about the family members you left behind. We are your family now. It is your duty to give yourselves to the mujahedeen, to serve them is to serve God. Now all of you repeat the Al-Shahadah after me. Once you repeat our creed, you will all be converted to our religion."

None of the women and girls dared not to repeat the Al-Shahadah except Sarah who stared at the moving lips around her. The arm of an ISIS guard yanked her from the crowd and pushed her forward to where the leader stood.

Panicked, Nazo ran after them. "She's my sister. She can't repeat your creed. She's mute."

The group leader gazed into Sarah's terrified face. He put his right hand on Sarah's head and chanted, "I witness that there is no God but Allah, and Mohammed is the Messenger of God." He grinned. "Now she's converted."

Nazo took Sarah's hand and disappeared into the crowd. ISIS fighters and the tribesmen who supported them drew girls by lottery. An ISIS fighter walked around the hall with a small notepad and a black plastic bag. He wrote down the women's names and dropped the slips into the bag. After the ISIS man noted down Nazo's name and threw it into the bag, he asked for Sarah's name.

WHAT COMES WITH THE DUST

"She's only eleven years old," Nazo protested.

The man stared at Sarah's small buds, visible like two halves of a tennis ball beneath her flowery dress. Then he turned to Nazo. "It is permissible to have intercourse with her before puberty if she's fit for it; if she's not, then it is enough to enjoy her body without intercourse," the man replied in a firm voice.

Nazo flashed the man her softest, most feminine smile before stating, "She is my first cousin, and her name is also Nazo."

The ISIS man's pupils dilated, as he again wrote the name Nazo and tossed it into the bag. "My name is Waleed," he added before he moved to the next girl.

Nazo held Sarah's hand in hers. Her pulse pounded like a drum in her ears as the rewarded ISIS fighters came forward to draw names from the bag. With each name, she breathed a sigh of relief, until she was overwhelmed by the selected girl's screams as some hungry man carried her off.

Viyan, the girl on Nazo's right, fought back and tried to slip from the hands of her new owner. He snatched her by the hair and dragged her to the door. Then he slammed her head against the doorframe till she passed out. Having subdued her, the man wiped his hands against his chest and removed Viyan's remaining hair from his thick fingers. Then he carried her through the door to the next room.

Nazo thanked God that Sarah was deaf and mute, unable to hear the screams of the girls in the next rooms where the ISIS men raped and beat them. Every hour or so, they brought some girls back to exchange them for others. Those who came back looked sickly, and their faces and bodies were covered with bruises. They said they had been injected with drugs and raped repeatedly.

An hour later, two ISIS men brought Viyan back to the basement. She could not walk and screamed in agonizing pain. Freshly dried blood stains were visible on the lower part of her pale blue gown. Nazo helped her to her feet and walked her to the toilet. On their way back from the toilet, Viyan stumbled, so Nazo placed a supporting hand under her arm.

"It wasn't just him," she told Nazo in a faint voice. "He gave me to four more fighters after he finished with me. Please, sister, help me to end this wretched life. Strangle me with your headscarf."

"You'll survive this—survive and have a good life again," Nazo assured her.

"They laughed at my weak body. They spat on my face each time one of them was done with me. They called me the ugly daughter of Satan. I hate myself! I hate this body!" she wailed.

Later that night Viyan crept into the bathroom. When she didn't return, Nazo followed. She found Viyan with a piece of cloth in her mouth to quiet her screams as she'd slit her veins with a shard of broken mirror. Her body shivered as she lay on the damp bathroom floor and waited for her soul to escape. With no other choice, Nazo simply closed the door and left the woman to her chosen fate.

In the morning, wailing girls circled Viyan's body. ISIS men wrapped her in a blanket and dragged her from the room to be thrown into the Tigris. The ISIS men ordered Nazo and another girl to clean the bathroom. The other girl opened the bathroom tap and wiped at the bloodstains on the floor while

Nazo gazed at the dozens of fingernail-sized black beetles plastered to the bathroom walls.

Nazo knelt against the bathroom wall and peeled the phone from her neck. She sighed as she gazed at the lifeless phone in her hand. When the other girl saw, she begged Nazo to give her the phone. She would call her brother, give him all details of their location so he could inform the Americans. "They'll bomb the building, erase every trace of this Hell from the Earth. It will put an end to our misery," she promised.

From that day, Nazo lived in constant fear that she or Sarah would be next. Most girls refused to eat; afraid the ISIS men had spiked the food they offered.

Girls stopped taking showers—some even smeared their clothes with excrement from the overflowing toilets to avoid being taken by the ISIS fighters and the slave buyers. Instead Nazo thought about a way to escape from the house. She talked with a young woman named Soleen and her friend Firmesk, who agreed to join her.

One afternoon they heard the roaring rumble of jet fighters followed by explosions nearby. ISIS guards ran from the room, and machine gun fire answered. Nazo took Sarah's hand in hers and signaled the other two girls to run. The four girls took the stairs two at a time to the first floor and dashed out the back door. Once they were in the yard, they rushed to the high concrete wall. There Nazo gave Sarah a leg up over the wall. Teetering on the uneven wall, Sarah slipped. She dropped to the street and landed with her left leg twisted at an impossible angle. The girl's face evinced the pain in her leg. Nazo hurried after her, followed by the other girls. She knelt down and lifted

Sarah in her arms. Then the four zipped along the empty street, with Nazo and Soleen supporting Sarah.

Under the barrage of anti-aircraft fire, Nazo heard the muffled noise of a car speeding toward them. She stepped into the street waving wildly. "My sister fell down the stairs when she heard the sound of the evil jets of the American infidels," she screamed as the car pulled to a stop.

The driver rushed out and helped Nazo lay Sarah into the backseat as the other girls climbed into the car. They zoomed off toward the general hospital on the other side of the bridge.

As the girls rushed through the hospital doors, the eyes of a guard followed them. "Why are you indecent and without a male escort?" he demanded.

Nazo realized that they had run from the house without even niqabs.

Then the ISIS guard asked for their identification cards.

"We were in such a rush! We forgot everything and hurried to the emergency room," Nazo claimed.

That seemed to satisfy him.

The doctors took Sarah for X-rays, then to the plastering room. Once the nurse finished plastering Sarah's leg, Waleed and two other ISIS fighters from the house burst into the room and herded the four girls outside to the parking lot.

Waleed frowned. "The taxi driver reported you. Severe punishment is awaiting you at the house."

"God forbid," Nazo gushed. "The girl fell down the basement stairs, and we took her over the wall, as the main gate was locked and you were busy fighting on the roof."

"I'd swear you're not an ordinary Yazidi girl. You're an undercover YBS." He winked as he referred to the newly formed Shingal Resistance Units. Before they got into the vehicle, he pulled Nazo aside. "Stick to your story when we arrive home, but I'm almost certain it won't work. Be prepared for a good whipping."

Once they arrived at the house, Abu Talha, the ISIS fighter in charge of the building, pushed the girls into the garden with Sarah still clinging to Nazo's neck and her plastered leg dangling over Nazo's arm. A man emerged with a black cable in his hand, and the three girls screamed for mercy at just the sight of him.

"Please," wailed Nazo, "let my sister go. She's already in great pain."

Waleed came forward and quietly told the commander, "This is a deaf and mute girl. She's unaware of what has happened. Sir, only the three evil girls should taste the lash."

Abu Talha yanked Sarah from Nazo's arms and handed her over to Waleed. Then Abu Talha waved his hand to the ISIS fighter.

That was Nazo's last clear sight before the lashing began. The cable landed everywhere except Nazo's face and she screamed for all she was worth. She screamed so loud she expected people at the end of the street could hear her. Her skin broke; her voice broke; her spirit broke. Soon she could do nothing but lie on the ground and wait for it to end. She knew she would limp more from the bruises and cuts for days.

After the session ended, they threw the three girls back into the basement so the other girls could see. Nazo's agony each time she saw Sarah's leg and the other two girls' stricken faces far exceeded the pain she felt from her bruised body.

Waleed smiled at her. "How's the YBS girl doing?"

"Thanks for what you did for Sarah."

"Everything has a price."

Nazo immersed herself in a fresh chain of thought. With Sarah's condition now, she would be off the auction block for some time, but escape became extremely difficult. Waleed might be a lifeboat for her and Sarah, but she had to arrange her thoughts and simmer her next scheme on a low fire.

"What do I owe you, Waleed?" she purred.

"You're a Muslim now. Marry me; be my devoted wife."

Nazo thought for a moment. "I'll marry you, but you have to pay my dowry as it is stated in Shari'a law."

"Do you want me to buy you a piece of gold or give you money?"

"My dowry is this." She pointed at Sarah.

"You want me to take care of the mute girl?"

"Just this once, then, I'll be yours forever."

"You mean—?"

"Yes, I want her out of here, back to Kurdistan."

Waleed frowned. "I'll see what I can do."

* * *

A few days later Waleed, escorted by two armed ISIS fighters, came down to the basement and called for the women to line up. Waleed took out his small notepad and began to write down the girls' names for his black bag.

When Waleed reached Nazo, he wrote down her name. In a slick move, he folded her name and slid his hand into the bag, but after he pulled it back, he slid the slip into his pocket before he moved to the next girl. He kept this up as weeks passed, at least two months but probably more, saving Nazo for his own reward. Each time Sarah remained lying on the floor, and Nazo watched her bite her nails and tilt her head to the side out of concern for the girls around them.

Long after she'd lost track of time, two men, giants in military fatigues, came down the basement stairs. They walked with sure steps and fierce glares toward the bag on the table. One of them put his hand into the bag, drew the first name, and gave it to Waleed. Nazo knew it wouldn't be her, but her heart burned in commiseration for other girls, whose anxiety was written on their faces.

"Firmesk Khalat!" shouted Waleed.

Firmesk collapsed to the floor sobbing as she heard her name. Like Nazo, she knew these were slave traders who wouldn't return her to the pool of *sabiyas*. Her friend Soleen ran to her and took her in her arms. As the second man stepped forward to pick a name, Soleen shouted, "There is no need for a second name; I will join Firmesk."

Nazo watched the two men heft the two girls over their shoulders and ascend the steps of the basement. All the other girls, including Nazo, raised their hands up and prayed that they would be safe.

Waleed drew near and assured Nazo, "Your prayers will be answered. We'll be married soon."

She managed a little smile at the corner of her mouth. "Oh, really?"

"I have arranged everything."

Nazo whispered, "When can she leave?"

"I have the approval to move you and the mute girl to another house for Yazidi girls. Instead, she'll be taken to Kurdish territory via Kirkuk."

"How about me?"

"You stay in the new house until I arrange for our marriage."

* * *

That Thursday, Waleed came to pick up Nazo and Sarah. He waited outside in the truck while Nazo carried Sarah in her arms up the stairs. They drove across the new bridge to the southwest part of the city. Waleed pulled over and opened the hood of the truck. Five minutes later a taxi parked behind them.

Waleed poked his head into the truck. "It's time to go."

Nazo carried Sarah to the backseat of the taxi. She leaned over her and rubbed her head. Then she placed a kiss on her forehead and got out. Waleed slammed the door of the taxi. Nazo's eyes moistened as she gazed at Sarah through the rear passenger window. Sarah tilted her head to the side and waved for Nazo to join her. Nazo stretched her hand through the half-open window. She curled her index finger and lowered her thumb, and Sarah did the same. Together their hands formed a heart shape. Then their heart split as the taxi roared away into the crowd of cars. Tears drenched her cheeks as Nazo got back into the truck. She couldn't tell if they were tears of joy or sorrow.

Once they arrived at the new house, Waleed led Nazo inside. "Don't worry about the lottery. Just be patient for a few days until I can find a proper place for us to live."

Around twenty Yazidi girls from different villages lived in that house. The girls told Nazo that they were also frequently raped and given away to fighters.

Nazo spotted a girl, thin and weak, lying on the floor, surrounded by a few others who rubbed her legs and arms. Every so often, this girl would wail in pain. Even as night fell, the girl continued to howl. Nazo leaned back against the wall and asked the girl next to her about the sick one.

"Sharmeen has cancer, but the guards refuse to take her to the hospital. They think she's faking to avoid being raped and sold."

A few sleepless nights later, Waleed visited Nazo.

"We will marry on Friday."

"One last favor before we marry?"

"What is it?" Waleed scratched his chin impatiently.

"There's a very sick girl in the house. She is in great pain. Could you arrange a visit for her to the hospital?"

"Nazo, my undercover girl, has turned into Mother Teresa." He ground his teeth.

"Do this for me, and I'll be your obedient wife forever after."

"I will look into it." Then he left.

The next morning, Waleed asked Nazo to bring Sharmeen outside. He had arranged for an appointment for her with a doctor in Mosul General Hospital. Nazo and another girl helped Sharmeen into the waiting car. Nazo, clad in a white niqab, and Sharmeen, clad in a black one, rode in the backseat to the hospital. Nazo and Waleed waited in the hallway while the doctor, clad in a blue niqab, came to take Sharmeen to the laboratory for blood tests. Then Nazo escorted her to the women's ward.

After long hours of waiting, the doctor approached Nazo and Waleed, who sat on a bench in the corridor. "Sharmeen has acute lymphoblastic leukemia." Nazo slipped from the corridor into the ward as the doctor told Waleed, "This girl is of no use to you anymore."

Sharmeen gazed at Nazo with her pale eyes. "Close the curtains. Let's exchange our niqabs, then run for your life."

Nazo shook her head. "I won't leave you."

Sharmeen took her hand and whispered, "I know my journey ends here. Yours has only begun."

Nazo slipped into the black niqab and helped Sharmeen into the white one. Nazo kissed her on her forehead, and they wished each other a safe trip into their futures. Nazo took a deep breath and grasped Sharmeen's hand. They both mumbled a quick prayer.

If she could reach the stairs at the end of the corridor, she could bolt for freedom. As she passed by Waleed sitting on a bench in the corridor, she prayed that he wouldn't recognize her walk with the slight limp. The stairs grew closer with each step.

As she descended the first few steps, she tripped over the hem of her long gown and tumbled the rest of the way to the landing. A few women in niqabs helped her to her feet. Nazo quickly dusted herself off and walked through the hall and then out the main door.

Once outside she slid into one of the many taxis lining the street by the hospital.

"Where to, sister?" the driver asked.

"The city center, brother." She closed her eyes and let her breath out in a puff.

WHEN THE shooting stopped, Omed remained perfectly still and silent. He lay face down, trapped under the body of the aged clergyman. Omed had been hit twice: once in his left leg and again in his chest. The old cleric had protected his head and chest. He stirred his stiff limbs as the trucks roared off and eased from under the man's dead body. Then he peeked around for any remaining ISIS fighters.

Satisfied they had gone, he crept among the bodies to check for survivors. As he reached Azad, a thick stream of blood ran down Azad's chest and his right hip, but he was still breathing. Omed knew he had only a short time before the ISIS men returned with a bulldozer to shove them into a mass grave, so he dragged Azad to the nearby orchard and hid with him among the olive trees.

With the help of his trusty blade, he cut strips from Azad's trousers and tied them around his gushing wounds. Then he removed Azad's leather belt and strapped it around Azad's chest to compress the bandages.

For his own bleeding leg, he stripped off his shirt and tied it over his wound. Then he raised his bloodstained hand and felt the bullet in his chest. He figured that the bullet must have passed through the body of the old cleric before it penetrated his torso and lodged in the muscle of his chest.

With a prayer that they would not bleed to death, Omed lay beside Azad and waited for the sun to go down. As the darkness crept into the sky, Omed hauled himself toward one of the neighboring villages to snatch a donkey to carry Azad during their journey to Mount Shingal.

He glimpsed a faint light in the distance coming from one of the houses at the rear of the village. When he drew closer to the house, a pack of dogs began barking. Exhausted, he stumbled and sank to his knees. The shorthaired dogs leaped at him. A beam of blinding light shone full on his face as he fought off the dogs that swarmed over him. With a few shouted commands from the man holding the flashlight, the dogs retreated toward the house. Omed fell to the ground panting; sweat dripped from his forehead onto his bleeding leg. The old man helped him to his feet and walked him into the house.

Inside, an old woman gave Omed a bottle of water. He downed it in one gulp. The couple helped dress his wounds, but Omed told them he needed to go back with a donkey to help a seriously wounded man in the olive orchard. The man agreed to loan him the donkey but refused to join him on the treacherous journey.

Omed took the rope dangling from the donkey's head and led him through the dark to the olive grove. He carefully shouldered Azad onto the back of the donkey, then headed back to the house. As he reached the foot of a small hill near the village, the headlights of pickup trucks loomed in the darkness. The growl of the vehicles startled the donkey, and Omed lost his grip on the rope. He threw himself into a nearby ditch. The agitated donkey went into a frenzy and ran into the beams of the trucks' headlights with Azad's body dangling from its back. Then a burst of gunfire erupted from an anti-aircraft machine gun mounted on the bed of a pickup. The donkey pitched forward and fell to the ground, lifeless. Azad's limp body rolled free and landed on a small rock at the foot of the hill.

Omed rose from his crouch, arm outstretched. His mouth opened as if to shout, though what he could have said, he had no idea. Helpless, he watched in the twin beams of the pickup as ISIS men riddled Azad's body with more bullets before they climbed back into their trucks.

Alone and numb, Omed waited till the trucks' taillights disappeared behind the other side of the hill, then he rose from the ground and began his miserable trek toward Mount Shingal. He walked for hours with his eyes set on the distant, craggy mass silhouetted in the dim moonlight.

He appreciated the searing pain in his leg. The sensation of pain gave him solace and the feeling that he wasn't alone. He wondered why he was running to the mountains. Why not lie down under the moonlight, enjoy the pain, and bleed to death? It was his biggest fear, that death would put an end to his pain.

The moonlight surrendered to the first light of the dawn, which spread down from the peaks of the mountain. Omed soon reached the base of the mountain. The instant he heard the trickling water of a nearby stream, he rolled his sticky tongue in his dry mouth. With an immense thirst clawing at his throat, he hurried toward the sound. Once there, he bent his head down to the small stream and drank deep until his thirst was quenched. He let the water flow over his head and face. Then he collapsed on his back by the stream.

Moments later, he heard the sound of small stones rolling down the slope toward his head. He tilted his head up and watched a group of armed men run down the mountain rocks toward him. Omed identified the men from their thick mustaches and red-checkered headdresses as Yazidi fighters from the Shingal Resistance Units, the YBS. He rose and let out a sigh of relief.

A man shouted at Omed and asked for his identification. He raised his empty hands and shouted back, "I'm a wounded Yazidi." The men then approached Omed and carried him to safety.

At the top of the mountain, they escorted him to the YBS emergency tent. A nurse dressed in khaki fatigues and a woodland camouflage vest that held half a dozen AK-47 magazines walked over to him. "I'm Soz." She helped him take off his damp, dirt-encrusted shirt and trousers. "Seems you were in a catfight before you got to the bullets," observed the nurse as she inspected the many scars on Omed's body.

"Yes, I woke up one morning from their yowling on my chest," Omed said with a grin.

"You have a cute smile, though."

Hearing this, Omed's thoughts flew back to the day when the melon had fallen from Nazo's basket. He thought of her and what might have happened to her at the hands of ISIS.

The nurse cleaned and dressed the wound on Omed's leg. Then she pressed her fingers against Omed's chest and felt the bullet between his ribs. "I'll bandage it for now, but this has to wait until you get to a hospital."

"Maybe I'll keep the bullet in my chest as a souvenir," Omed teased.

A jolt ran through his body as Soz prodded around the bullet once more. "You're a lucky guy. That bullet must have gone through another body before it lodged in you."

"Yes, an old Yazidi cleric."

"Ta'us Malik saved you."

"Oh, you are Yazidi?"

"Yes, I am."

A haggard woman appeared at the tent flap with a weakened child. Soz walked over to her and helped her to place the child on the folding table. She gave the mother a half-liter of bottled water, possibly enough to keep the child alive another day. The woman raised her hands to the sky in appreciation and left.

Drinking water was more precious than gold on the slopes of Shingal Mountain. The nurse told Omed that around forty children had died from dehydration and exhaustion in the past two days. Her eyes glistened with tears as she told Omed how helpless she felt. "This is the only medical tent for the forty-thousand people who fled here. I only have some bandages and a few bottles of water."

Aware that others were waiting, Omed ignored his thirst and shambled outside. A sheen of sweat coated his body as he walked in the blazing heat of the afternoon sun. He struggled to find himself a patch of shade among the thousands of strained faces scattered along the bare mountain slopes. Near a group of people that huddled at the entrance of a small cave, he found a space to sit on the ground.

Omed craved an afternoon nap. As his eyelashes drooped, the muffled sound of a helicopter whirled in his head. Suddenly the exhausted people around him burst into a hopeful, desperate, panicked stampede as the thunderous helicopter circled over their heads. They ran toward it and stretched their hands for the airdropped relief supplies. Minutes later, the crowds swarmed the helicopter as it landed to take a few families aboard.

The pilot took off unaware that an old man clung to a landing skid of the helicopter. When it neared three hundred feet in the air, Omed watched the old man's red-and-white checkered headscarf twirl down to the ground. Moments later, the old man lost his faint grip and fell on the northern slopes.

* * *

The next morning Omed woke with a stiff neck from the stone he'd used as a pillow. He sat on a rock overlooking a cliff. As he tried to tilt his head to the side, his neck shrieked in protest. Yet the pain in his neck and his leg didn't offer the relief, the thrill, that he needed. He rolled his tongue around and pulled the razor blade from his mouth. He drew the razor close to his face and studied it. Through the three holes of the blade,

Omed watched the smoke rise from the houses in the town of Shingal.

His body itched with the tremendous urge, the need, to carve new cuts. He pressed the razor to his chest, yet before he slid the blade down, he remembered that Soz, the YBS nurse, wanted to change his bandages today. Imagining how she would tease him for his new cuts, he drew back and threw the razor into the air. He watched it travel down the side of the steep cliff, and felt as if his heart had left his body and fallen with it. A voice in his mind urged him to walk to the YBS emergency tent. He didn't know if it was the need to quench his thirst, the comforting shade from the relentless sun, or his desperate need for human contact.

Omed waited his turn among the women carrying their mewling children and the old men supported by younger men at the half-open tent flap. As he entered the tent, he jerked back his head and raised his eyebrows when he found a male medic inside. The man told Omed that Soz had gone to the Syrian side of the border to procure medicine and supplies.

That afternoon, an Iraqi Army helicopter dropped some humanitarian supplies on the northern slopes. Omed ran toward the supply drop, favoring his wounded leg, but he stumbled to the ground. As so many people fought to scramble aboard the helicopter, a husband and wife lifted their two little daughters over their heads and rushed into the crowd. They threw their precious girls over the heads of other desperate people into the helicopter.

The overweight helicopter took off, shuddering in its ascent. Aloft only a few moments, it crashed into the rocks. The parents of the two girls ran screaming toward the crushed helicopter. A crowd of people pulled out the dead body of the pilot. The husband rushed into the helicopter, then emerged with his two daughters on his shoulders, alive with minor injuries.

Helpless and lost, Omed hauled himself to his feet. He walked past a group of fresh graves. Unable to dig into the rocky mountainside, the displaced people buried their loved ones in shallow graves and covered their bodies with stones. He fought the urge to vomit at the smell of the rotting bodies of the children and the elderly. Those who had died were relieved of the horrors of the unrelenting heat and thirst and from the terror of being slaughtered by ISIS fighters, who surrounded the mountain on all sides.

Still, when he saw Soz inside the medical tent, a smile lit Omed's face. Soz talked with him as she changed the bandages on his leg. The new packs of bottled water in the corner of the tent caught Omed's eye. He needed a bottle like the desert needed early rain, but the tiny graves on the mountainside forbade him from asking. Instead, he turned to Soz and asked if she had a cigarette.

She reached into her baggy trousers and pulled out two. "Let's go outside for a smoke. There are two things we will never run out of: ISIS fighters and cigarettes."

"And the third thing is women freedom fighters," Omed joked as they left the tent.

"I bet, if it weren't for us, ISIS would control the world."

"If women took up arms, they would control the world."

Soz grinned. "If women controlled the world, there would be no wars—"

"I've heard that before—just a bunch of jealous countries not talking to each other." Omed laughed. "Is it true that ISIS fighters avoid combat with women?"

"They think if they're killed by a woman, they won't be considered martyrs of God and won't enter Heaven."

Omed chuckled. "So women fighters prevent ISIS men from enjoying their seventy-two virgin maids after their death?"

"Yes, but we can't stop them from raping our girls."

Disgust crept into her eyes. "Imagine if Yazidi women had known how to use arms! They could have defended themselves and prevented what happened to them."

My beloved Nazo. "What has ISIS done with them?"

Soz snorted. "Spoils of war, traded as sex slaves."

Anger simmered in Omed's veins. "Can I join the YBS?"

"Yes, but your leg needs to heal. Know anything about first aid? You can be my assistant."

"No, but I'm good at carving human skin; I might end up as a slick plastic surgeon."

"Nice. I need some work on my nose."

Omed shook his head. "No, you're perfect; you don't need any work."

After a moment of uncomfortable silence, she asked, "Do you have anyone out there? Kidnapped by ISIS?"

"No, I lost everyone in my family a few years back."

"So you're alone here?"

"I'm far from alone, but I am lonely. How about you?"

Soz took a deep drag from her cigarette and told her story:

"I attended the nursing school in Dohuk, and I used to come back to my village on summer holiday to help on my family's farm. A couple of weeks back, I was working at our melon fields nearby. There I heard the big Humvee engines followed by a burst of gunfire, then women's screams. I grabbed my small mattock and ran as fast as I could.

"When I reached a safe distance, I called my family. They told me that ISIS had surrounded them; they couldn't get out of the village. They pleaded with me to run for my life to the foot of Shingal mountain. After an hour of walking, I called my family again, kept redialing until the battery died, but there was no answer. When a trail of dust sprawled in the distance, indicating some truck speeding toward me, I ran again. The truck just circled me like a vulture. Then it came to a stop. From the cloud of dust emerged an armed man with his face covered by a black balaclava.

"I hid the mattock behind my back and stood still. He stared at me for a moment—his eyes filled with desire. I recognized him, Nashwan, an Arabian boy from a neighboring village who used to harass me in secondary school. He wanted me to convert and elope with him. Instead, I reported him to the headmaster, and they expelled him from school. He must have been looking for me in the village, and when he didn't find me there, he simply headed to the farm. That son of a motherless goat, Nashwan, stood in front of me, now dressed in Afghani garb with an ISIS flag behind his head, flapping from his huge vehicle, a rifle in his hands. I tightened my grip on the mattock behind my back as he approached. When he raised his arm to grab me, I plunged the mattock into his chest. He fell to the ground and dropped the rifle. I picked it up and ran toward the truck.

"Since I was fourteen, I'd driven a tractor for my father, so I drove away, toward the foot of the mountain, until I came across of a group of YBS fighters. They started shooting at me, since I hadn't thought to take down the ISIS flag from the top of the truck. Bullets struck the front wheels and fenders.

"Before the truck came to a halt, I jumped out the door, rolled on the ground, and landed on my belly.

"The fighters approached, shouting, 'It's an ISIS suicide attack.'

"'I'm a Yazidi Kurd! Don't shoot! Don't shoot!' I shouted back.

"A few of the women lifted me from the ground. They searched me for explosives while the men headed to the truck and raised the hood in search of anything suspicious.

"The man in charge picked up the assault rifle from the seat and walked toward me while I guzzled water from a bottle one of the women had given me. 'A Yazidi woman with a gun in an ISIS truck? What's your story?'

"I told them everything.

"The older man handed me the assault rifle and the keys to the Humvee. 'You should be proud. You are among the first Yazidi women fighters against the Daesh.' Hearing this, I wanted to cry.

"The women came forward, and they all hugged me. One pointed to the nearby Shrine of Sharfadeen. She said they thought I was a suicide bomber who was targeting the holy place.

"As I entered the open courtyard of the holy shrine, I took off my shoes and stooped to go through the arched passage to the inner chamber. I kissed the stone wall before entering. Then I picked up a swath of green silk hanging on the wall and tied my knot. I closed my eyes and made my only wish— to see my sister Soleen again. Before I left the dimness of the room, I knelt and reached down to the small hole in the floor and brought up some sacred soil in my fingertips. I prayed for Xuda, the Supreme God, and dabbed the soil on my forehead for a blessing.

"The holy shrine became a safe haven for the displaced Yazidi families, who took refuge in the temple as in the ancient Yazidi prophecy. A group of Yazidi Peshmerga protecting the shrine came forward and asked me to join them. I told them the YBS had found me first.

"For a few days, I did join in on fighting missions, but the YBS knew about my nursing experience and asked me to help the displaced people here on the mountainside.

"A couple of days later, I received the news that ISIS had killed most of the people from my village, including my father and my two younger brothers. They took Soleen, my thirteen-year-old sister.

"I will never forget. I will never forgive. I promised myself I won't die until I see my sister again, until we go home. I killed my heart, turned it into a small rock in my chest. All day I played tough in front of everyone, but when I remembered my family and what might have happened to Soleen at the hands of ISIS, I went behind a rock and cried until the others shouted for me to come and join the group dance before our next mission."

NAZO WALKED aimlessly through the old town of Mosul. What to do next? She didn't dare ask anyone for help.

The sun kissed the horizon, and darkness crept over the city. She leaned against a wall in one of the narrow alleys to rest her fatigued legs and hopefully to collect her scattered thoughts.

A white-haired old man passed by and stood at the door to the nearest house. He held a bag of tomatoes in one hand and knocked at the door with the other. Before he could disappear inside the house, Nazo ran over and threw herself at his feet.

"I beg you, sir, I need shelter for the night."

"Are you a non-Muslim?" he asked.

"Yes," Nazo admitted in a desperate voice.

"Move along, woman. I don't want any trouble."

"Please, sir, I implore you, give sanctuary and hospitality to a stranded woman as is the Arabian tradition."

The old man shook his head from side to side. "A tradition once, perhaps, but not anymore."

"You're not going to let me in?"

"No," he replied firmly. "I don't want my old flesh to burn from my bones while I'm locked in a cage in the town square because of you."

Nazo buried her face in her hands and sobbed. "Then at least promise me you won't report me."

"You have my word." In shame, he turned his head from her desperate face. He slipped inside and silently closed the door behind him.

Nazo shivered when the cool night wind blew through her dress. Her toes peeked out of the holes in her shoes as she walked through the dimly lit alleys.

She arrived at an old mosque in time for the *maghrib* prayer. She stood at a street corner opposite the mosque door. A few minutes later, the men inside the mosque began to flow out.

Nazo hurried across the street before the Muslim priest locked the door. She clung to the iron bars of the mosque gate. "Mullah, I ask for sanctuary in God's house."

"Are you a beggar or gypsy?"

"No, I'm a new convert."

"What do you want, woman?"

"I need shelter for the night."

"Daughter, a woman cannot sleep in a mosque without a male relative."

"Then take me to your house. I'll leave very early in the morning."

WHAT COMES WITH THE DUST

"I can't do that, but stay here a moment." He went inside and came back with an autumn coat, a loaf of bread and some cheese. He gave them to her through the gate. "You have to leave now before one of them comes."

Nazo gratefully slid into the man's coat. She devoured the bread and cheese, then resumed her shamble through the dark streets. Her tired legs stopped aching and merely drifted along below her body as she strode the empty street. Shadows covered the ground as the fog thickened. Then, through the fog emerged a young man who stood at the gate to a house, smoking. A haze of blue cigarette smoke disappeared into the white fog. The young man hid his lit cigarette stealthily under his coat sleeve as she passed by. Nazo walked faster when she heard the sound of footsteps behind her growing closer.

"Do you need help, sister?"

Nazo turned to the voice. "I'm lost."

"A runaway?"

Nazo nodded.

"Follow me," the young man instructed. "You've found the right person."

He dropped his cigarette on the ground and crushed the butt under his shoe. He turned, led her through a nearby gate, and knocked at a small wooden door.

An old man opened the door. "A hundred times I've told you not to stay out after dark."

"I was praying at the mosque."

"*You? Praying at the mosque?!* I'm your father, not some ISIS *hezbah* policeman. Get in here." Over the young man's

81

shoulder, the old man noticed Nazo. "And who is this woman with you?"

"Father, close the door, and I'll tell you."

Once they were inside, the young man guided Nazo to the kitchen. An old woman stood over the kerosene stove cooking rice. The smell of boiled rice caught Nazo's attention as she dropped her exhausted body onto a wooden bench.

"Who is this woman?" the lady of the house asked.

"She's a Yazidi girl," the son answered.

"I don't recall either you or your father fighting for ISIS, so who bestowed this gift upon you?"

"She fell from the sky," said the son.

"So, did she fall for you or for that old sack of dead meat?" She pointed to her husband.

The old man shouted at his son, "Are you out of your mind? Do you want my head impaled on a post in the city center tomorrow?"

"I would love to see that," the old woman replied.

The young man drew closer to the older one and whispered in his ears. "Father, a *sabiya* means money."

The old man's eyes widened. "Do what you want, but I want no part in this!"

The woman put some warm rice on a small plate and gave it to Nazo. "You must be ill-fated. Of all the men in Mosul, you came across this useless son of a dickless father."

"Shut your mouth, woman. If I'm dickless, where did your son come from?"

"For God's sake, stop it," the young man chided.

"Shut your mouths both of you, and move your feet instead. Go out and find yourselves jobs." The woman shook her wooden spoon at them as she spoke.

"Where are the jobs?" asked the father.

"Join ISIS," the old woman suggested.

"I don't have the skills; I can't shoot like them anymore," the old man admitted.

"You don't have to tell me. I know you aren't shooting bullets anymore," the old woman clucked.

While the old husband and wife continued bickering, Nazo enjoyed her meal. Warm and fed, she fell into a dreamless slumber at the table.

Early in the morning, Nazo woke to the voice of the young man. He paced the kitchen floor, back and forth, talking on his mobile phone. The mother stirred what smelled like eggs in a rusty frying pan.

Nazo headed outside to the open toilet near the main gate. As she came out, she tiptoed to the main exit and slipped her hand around the doorknob. Her lips pulled into a grimace against her teeth when she failed to turn the knob. It rattled, but the door wouldn't open. They had locked the door on her.

She walked back to the kitchen.

"Have something to eat. We leave in ten minutes."

"Where to?" asked Nazo.

"Mount Shingal," the young man replied.

Nazo froze in place, then she hurried to the table and devoured the two scrambled eggs like a wolf while the old woman watched in distress.

At a knock on the door, the young man stood from his chair and beckoned for Nazo to follow him.

"All right," a friend of the young man said, "you can borrow my car and my sister's identification, but bring them both back in one piece."

Nazo and the young man set off on the main road to Shingal. As each mile passed, her heart beat faster. After an hour and a half, Nazo gazed through the car window at the grand old mountain. Shingal loomed in the distance.

"We can't drive closer to the mountain because of the ISIS patrols," the young man cautioned.

"Get me as close as you can; I'll gladly walk the rest of the way," Nazo replied, excited to rejoin her sister.

"No, I have a better plan. I'll hand you over to a man. When the sun rises, he will escort you to the foot of the mountain."

They reached the town of Shingal and continued to a farmhouse on the outskirts. At the large gate, the young man pressed on the car horn. Moments later, a man appeared at the gate to let them in.

A tall, dark man clad in a white Afghani outfit and a vest that held rifle magazines received them in the farmyard. Nazo watched the dark man give a small envelope to the young man, who got back into the car and roared away through the main gate.

Nazo turned to the dark man. "Sir, what time will we depart for the mountain?"

"What mountain?" sneered the dark man. "I bought you from that guy on the condition that you're still a virgin, and you'd better be."

Nazo struggled to stay on her feet. The world around her spun faster and faster. Her vision blurred as if a big hammer had smacked her head, and she toppled to the ground.

Moments later, splashes of water hit her face. She opened her eyes. A guard carried Nazo to a room at the rear of the farmhouse. The room was dimly lit from a small, fortified window high overhead. He threw her on the floor and locked the heavy metal door.

Disheartened, Nazo sat up and pressed her face to the wall. When a hand tapped her shoulder, she turned back to see two girls crouched over her.

Too forlorn to form words, Nazo pressed her back against the wall and let her head loll. She tucked her knees to her chest, wrapped her arms around them, and tried not to cry.

"Nazo, it's us. Don't you remember?" called one of the girls.

Nazo raised her head and stared at the two smiling faces of Firmesk and Soleen. She spread her arms and hugged the two girls. The three burst into tears. Firmesk told Nazo that they were now the property of Abu Salma, an ISIS slave dealer.

In the afternoon, a guard unlocked the door and took Firmesk to the main building to do the cooking, washing, and house cleaning.

Soleen walked to the corner of the room and picked up a plastic five-gallon bucket. She flipped the bucket over and placed it under the window. Then she jumped on the bucket, and as she stared through the iron bars, she waved for Nazo to come and join her. There was barely enough room for one, but Nazo clasped Soleen's shoulder, pulled herself behind her, and threw her arms around the other woman's waist.

GHARBI M. MUSTAFA

They both gazed at nearby Mount Shingal.

"Do you have someone up there?" asked Nazo.

"All I have is there—my elder sister, Soz, a nurse." Soleen's face clenched. "I mean, if she made it through."

Nazo tightened her hands around Soleen's waist. "I'm sure she did."

"How about you?"

"My heart is there," Nazo answered.

"With who?" Soleen smiled

"Dr. Azad."

"Oh, you have a heart problem?"

"Yes, and he's the only one who can treat it."

They both laughed.

The two girls heard a crack and felt the plastic give until the bucket collapsed under their feet. They both fell to the floor, still laughing.

A couple of hours later, Firmesk came back with some rice and soup in Styrofoam bowls. As the girls ate, Nazo asked Firmesk if she could smuggle a knife or some rat poison from the kitchen next time.

"Nazo, you never give up, do you?" Soleen chuckled.

"Enough of your James Bond schemes! I'm not in this time!" Firmesk laughed heartily. "I'm still bruised from the beating at the Mosul house."

The girls' laughter stopped when they heard the rattle of a key in the lock.

The guard took Nazo, led her through the house, then pushed her into a room where Abu Salma sat cross-legged on a foam mattress—the only furnishing in the long hall. He stood and grabbed Nazo by the throat. He pulled a pistol from the leather holster at his waist and placed the tip of the barrel right against Nazo's forehead.

Nazo felt the chill of the muzzle on her flesh.

"I have a special customer for you. Tell me the truth, are you still a virgin?" the dark man asked.

Nazo blinked. "Yes."

Abu Salma shouted to one of the two guards to get the truck ready. He yanked Nazo by her arms and shoved her into the truck. Nazo's heart sank when they arrived at the hospital. Once inside, Abu Salma put his finger on the trigger of his M-16 rifle and ordered the doctor to perform a virginity examination on Nazo. The doctor asked in a polite voice for him to wait outside the room. After he had performed the examination and blood tests, Nazo knew what awaited her, as the doctor didn't dare to hide the truth.

"Sir, this girl isn't a virgin; she's pregnant."

Before Nazo could react to that news, Abu Salma yanked her off her feet and began pummeling her with his fists. Nazo broke free and hid behind the doctor, who spread both his arms in an effort to protect her. Abu Salma shoved the doctor to the floor. Then he leaped on her, knocking her to the ground.

As Abu Salma rested all his weight on her womb, the doctor shouted, "You're gonna kill her; you're gonna kill her!" He rose from the ground and pushed the slave trader off her.

Since the trader had poured all his anger out on her already, Abu Salma sat behind the doctor's desk and lit a cigarette. Soon he stood and squashed the cigarette under his heel. Then, as Nazo whimpered, he dragged her limp body from the hospital and across the parking lot. The gravel tore through her niqab and ripped at her bare legs until they reached his car.

Along the road back to the farm, while Abu Salma listened to loud ISIS hymns on the car radio, Nazo cried in silence. All of her body ached, and she feared he'd broken a bone under her eye.

Once the car arrived at the farm gate, Abu Salma pressed the horn, and a guard opened the gate. Since Nazo was too weak to stand, one of the guards carried her into the barred room and threw her onto the thin, checkered mattress. She laid her head on a pink pillow embroidered with a red flower and two green leaves.

In a few moments, her tears stopped, and a smile curved her lips as she imagined herself carrying a blue-eyed baby in her arms, blue eyes like Azad's. At that moment, there were billions of voices flying across the universe, but she was immersed in the thought of her baby's first laugh. The giggles breathed life into her, and that alone was reason enough to live.

Then her face clouded as the color of the baby's eyes turned to black and a long beard trailed down the baby's bare chest. After eating, she hid a plastic plate under her dress and asked the girls to help her to the tiny bathroom in the corner. She pulled the filthy curtain closed. Moments later, the two girls yanked back the curtain, obviously having heard the sound of the breaking plate followed by Nazo's muted wail.

Angry and frustrated, Nazo sat on the floor as blood dripped from her wrist. The broken plastic wasn't sharp enough; the cut was shallow and ragged.

When the girls kicked on the door and shouted for help,

two guards rushed in. They took Nazo to the house and bandaged her wrist.

Abu Salma lunged at her. "I've already lost a lot of money on you! Do you wanna die? Really, do you want to die?" He pulled out his berretta and handed it over to Nazo. "Go ahead. Join your Satan in the fires of Hell."

Stunned, grateful, Nazo took the gun from his hand like a precious treasure. She placed the barrel in her mouth and pulled the trigger.

The gun merely clicked.

Abu Salma fell into a fit of laughter. "I swear, you're from the Shingal Resistance Units."

The next morning at six, Abu Salma walked into the room holding three clean gowns and niqab headdresses. He told the girls to bathe and slip into their new clothes. He allowed them a bit of privacy but left the room door open.

Half an hour later, the girls were led outside. Nazo saw two shiny cars waiting in the farmyard. An overweight man in a Muslim cleric's outfit got out of his car and opened the rear door while two of the guards dragged Firmesk into his car. He roared away through the main gate with Soleen running behind the car screaming for her friend.

Two ISIS fighters with long beards got out of the other vehicle and ran after Soleen. They caught her by the neck and dragged her into the other car. Then they came for Nazo, who started to walk toward the car before they forced her. She sat in the rear seat, hugged Soleen, and then pulled the distraught girl's head to her lap. Nazo's thighs grew moist from Soleen's ceaseless tears. The two men high-fived each other and climbed into the car. The one who took the driver's seat was tall with a prominent nose, and the second was almost as tall with bushy eyebrows. The two men spoke in a North African Arabic accent.

They drove west toward the Iraqi-Syrian border. Along the road, Nazo saw many ISIS fighters, their flags flapping over the conquests of their battles. After a six-hour drive, they arrived at an abandoned house that overlooked the Euphrates River.

After they drove into the compound, Bushy Eyebrows locked the main gate behind them. They pushed the two girls into the house and went back to the car. Soleen huddled in the corner of the room and tucked her head between her knees. Nazo pulled the curtain open a crack so she could watch the two men wielding big screwdrivers to remove panels from the side doors and trunk. They pulled out many packs of bank-notes and threw them into a large cardboard box. Once they were done, they walked back and sat on the threshold. Nazo moved away from the window and tiptoed behind the door to hear their conversation.

"These two girls are very tempting," said the fighter with the prominent nose.

"Remember, we're transporters—we can't touch the merchandise," said Bushy Eyebrows.

"Maybe we can't touch the money, but we can have some fun with the two Yazidi girls before delivering them to their owners," said Prominent Nose.

"Sleeping with them is an act of good." Bushy Eyebrows chuckled at his own joke.

"In this mortal life as in Heaven," Prominent Nose added.

WHAT COMES WITH THE DUST

"God forbid these filthy mongrels ever enter Heaven." He let out a snort. "Besides, we won't need them. God willing, the seventy-two virgin *hoories* await us."

Prominent Nose interlaced his hands behind his head and leaned against the wall. "Doe-eyed heavenly maids with round, perky breasts. The *hoories* have transparent skin. You can see through to the marrow of their bones."

Bushy Eyebrows' eyes widened. "I heard they restore their virginity after each time you sleep with them."

There was silence, then both sighed. Moments later they mumbled a few words, and Nazo heard a coin drop on the concrete stoop.

"Ah, the younger one is mine, the intelligent one yours," shouted Bushy Eyebrows.

Nazo backed away from the door as she heard their footsteps approaching. The men walked into the room. Bushy Eyebrows' arm reached like a tentacle to wrap tightly around Nazo's throat, and he dragged her to sit by the wall across from the TV set. Then Prominent Nose yanked Soleen from her feet and dragged her to the wall beside Nazo.

He turned to the TV set. "Let's watch something as a warm-up before we get to the action." He laughed as he inserted a disk into the DVD player and then wedged himself between the two women.

Nazo cringed at the sight of a machete on the screen, then retched as she watched the video of men's severed heads staring from inside cooking pots. The scene shifted to a shot of ISIS men standing victorious with one foot on more severed heads.

She didn't wipe the puke from her lap in the hope that would leave the two men disgusted. The smell of fresh vomit permeated the room. Then Prominent Nose stood, ripped off Nazo's dress, and threw it outside the room.

Soleen screamed and buried her face in her hands. Bushy Eyebrows cupped her head from behind and forced her to watch the remaining video. "Watch," he coaxed. "They are your fellow Yazidis. You might recognize some of the heads."

When the horror show ended, Bushy Eyebrows yanked Soleen to her feet and dragged her to the next room.

"Don't mess too much with the merchandise; I don't want any trouble getting paid!" shouted Prominent Nose.

Nazo felt sick again. She stood to run to the bathroom, but Prominent Nose grabbed her by the hair. He chopped his right hand into Nazo's throat and then pushed her against the fortified window. He took off his leather belt and used it to secure Nazo's wrists to the window bars.

From the nightstand, he took out a syringe and an ampoule. Nazo tried with all her remaining strength to release her hands as she watched him stick the needle into the bottle and fill the syringe. Leering, he knelt by Nazo and plunged the needle into her thigh.

When he looked up to meet Nazo's eyes, she spat on his face. He unfastened the belt and threw Nazo on the bed. From the other room, Soleen screamed, "Stop it, please! Stop it! It hurts!"

The last thing Nazo saw was a distorted image of Prominent Nose floating naked over her body, trying to shove his large toes into her mouth.

Nazo fell into a heavy sleep. She dreamed she was sailing up the Tigris River in a small rowboat. From the thick fog emerged an old bridge. As she drew closer, Nazo saw a woman in a white gown, her face covered by a niqab, running on the bridge. When she reached the middle, she climbed the side wall. Then she pulled her niqab over her head and let it go. It whirled in the air before it caught on the iron bars at the end of the bridge.

A chill ran through Nazo when she recognized the young girl's pale face. It was Sharmeen, the sick girl from the house in Mosul. She stood erect with her hairless head and skinny body on the old bridge wall. Two nurses and an ISIS guard from the hospital ran toward her. Soft raindrops hit Nazo's face as she raised her head up and stretched her arms toward Sharmeen. Nazo let out a piercing scream as she watched Sharmeen spread her skinny arms in the air and let herself fall into the Tigris. The freezing waters of the river wrapped around her, and she disappeared into the murky depths before Nazo could reach her.

While the current pulled the rowboat downriver, Nazo buried her face in her hands and prayed for the girl. The rough waters and her powerful grief racked her with pain. Her belly cramped and coiled as if someone had stabbed her stomach with a serrated blade. As she scrambled to her feet to jump into the river and end her misery, she felt something between her legs struggling to be free of her body. She crouched while her yells filled the air. In moments, a bluish infant, covered in blood, fell to the deck of the boat. Before Nazo could reach her baby, a flock of gulls swarmed the boat. They plucked up the newborn but dropped it into the water.

Nazo blinked and rubbed her eyes. Hot drops of liquid fell on her neck, and a thin arm curved around her waist. She turned her head back to see a smile on Soleen's sobbing face. Nazo threw her arms around her neck, and they both sobbed. Their tears fell on the same pillow.

Prominent Nose and Bushy Eyebrows high-fived each other as they walked into the room, agreeing to swap girls. Bushy Eyebrows yanked Nazo from the bed and dragged her toward the other room as Prominent Nose snaked his left arm around Soleen's neck and pulled her backward off the bed. She fell to her knees and clung to Nazo's ankles. No matter how desperately they clung to each other, they couldn't prevent the men from prying them apart.

Nazo closed her eyes as Bushy Eyebrows rose on top of her. When he knelt down to enter her, he heard Prominent Nose cursing and yelling for him to come back. Nazo stood and ran behind him. She froze, then let out a piercing wail as she saw Soleen lying naked on the bed.

So still, so very still.

Nazo threw herself on the bed and embraced Soleen. Her body was cool, and her breathing was slow and shallow. She kept whispering, "Soz . . . Soz . . ." A few moments later, her eyes dilated and her breathing stopped.

"You animals! Take her to the hospital!" Nazo screamed.

Bushy Eyebrows checked Soleen's neck for a pulse. He gazed at the morphine syringe lying on the floor, then signaled to Prominent Nose. They yanked Soleen from Nazo's embrace again, wrapped her in a blanket, and carried her from the room. Nazo hurried behind them, but they pushed her back into the room and locked the door. Nazo hurried to the window and watched the two men walk down the small hill. They threw Soleen, barely alive, into the Euphrates River.

As the two men pushed the door open, Nazo leaped on Prominent Nose like a wildcat and dug her fingernails into his face and neck. Bushy Eyebrows yanked her free and dragged her toward the other room, but Prominent Nose tried to snatch Nazo's hair over his shoulder.

"You've already done enough damage!" Bushy Eyebrows growled at him. "Let's just deliver this girl and pray to Allah that the other girl's buyer doesn't want our heads." Bushy Eyebrows shoved Prominent Nose back. Then he gripped Nazo's hands behind her back, secured them with zipping ties, and led her outside. There, he threw her into the rear seat of the SUV, and soon they hit the road.

The SUV arrived at a house in the northern suburb of Raqqa. Two armed men stood at the entrance of the house. Bushy Eyebrows pulled Nazo out of the back and cut her numb hands free while Prominent Nose picked up the cardboard box full of money, and the three walked into the house.

A man with large feet in white socks and a checkered headdress appeared in his living room. His black beard trailed from his frowning face.

"Sir, we brought the revenues and the Yazidi *sabiya*," said Prominent Nose, handing the box to the man who signaled to the two men, and both withdrew from the room.

The man looked Nazo up and down, seemingly indifferent. "You are here to take care of my house and cook for my men," he said in his Egyptian accent, one she knew well from the Egyptian soap operas on TV. Then the man fixed his gaze on Nazo. "You will also take care of my daughter. She is possessed by a jinn. She poured hot water on a jinn lying on the bathroom floor and forgot to utter Allah's name."

Then he led Nazo upstairs to a room on the second floor. In the dim light, a girl in her early teens, with long dark-brown hair dangling down her shoulders, sat on the edge of her bed facing the curtained window. The girl didn't rise or move as Nazo and her father approached.

"This is your new servant, a Yazidi girl, who'll be part of your dowry. Since she worships Satan and you're possessed by him, you should make a perfect match. She can sleep on a pallet on your floor," the man proclaimed before he left the room.

Nazo sat on a chair and stared at the girl, remembering the story her grandmother used to tell her when she was a little girl: "Nazo, all my life I was an obedient wife to your grandfather because he was on good terms with a local jinn, and I was afraid, if I annoyed him, he would set his jinn on me. He told me that, one afternoon while he sat on a rock at the slopes of Mount Shingal and blew his flute for the sheep to chew better, he noticed one of the sheep had been stolen by a wolf. Your grandpa called out for his jinn friend for help. There was a popping sound that startled the sheep, and a voice cried out, 'Wolf, restore him his sheep!' So, the wolf meekly returned his sheep."

In that moment, Nazo prayed and implored her grandpa's soul to call upon his jinn to return her to Mount Shingal and save her from these crows of the desert, these black-eyed ISIS men.

Soon an idea came to Nazo. *If she speaks to jinn, she might be able to summon a jinn who can tell me the color of my baby's eyes.*

She gathered her courage and walked to the girl. "Salaam, I'm Nazo," she said formally with a deep bow before she reached forward for a handshake.

Instead of introducing herself, the girl turned her gaze to Nazo, her deep, distinctly purple eyes sparkling below the frown that furrowed her thin eyebrows. Her skin was unlike anything Nazo had seen before, ghostly pale like a porcelain doll. The girl's anger and misery hung in the air like a veil that draped over everything in the room.

Startled, certain the girl must be possessed, Nazo withdrew her hand and hurried downstairs. Work awaited her, and she buried herself in the effort of cleaning and cooking, not thinking of what might happen in the night. Thankfully, the girl with the wild eyes was fast asleep by the time Nazo climbed the stairs again. Tired, she was glad to see that the girl had laid out a thick pad of bedding for her and a single thin pillow, just enough to be comfortable.

The next morning Nazo woke before the girl. After fixing breakfast for the men and cleaning up the kitchen, she prepared a tray laden with tahini, a cup of tea, and a loaf of bread. She carried it to the girl's room.

The girl stood in front of her oval mirror and glared at her own reflection. A huge mass of thick, wild, untamed brown hair surrounded her shimmering white face like a tatted mane. Nazo peeked out the corner of her eye at the girl's face, reflected in the mirror, gazing back at her while she put the tray on the small table. When Nazo turned to flee, the girl spoke over her shoulder. "I know about your burden." That made Nazo freeze. "You're carrying a forbidden child."

Nazo stepped toward the girl, her throat dry with apprehension. "Is there a way to know the color of his eyes?"

"You're lucky: today's Tuesday, a good day for summoning the jinn."

She sat on the table and closed her eyes while Nazo stood in the far corner of the room watching in anticipation. The food tray shook on the table. The sound of the teaspoon hitting the edge of the teacup filled the air. Then the girl started speaking a language Nazo had never heard before. Nazo's ears stayed on alert but couldn't pick out any words from the exchange the young girl made with herself except 'jinn.'

After a long moment of silence, the girl turned to Nazo. "It's Mawtalic, the language of the dead."

"Could you see the color of his eyes?"

"The being inside you has no eyes color yet, but the soul of a dead person has entered you. Your child is alive and healthy, and the jinn says that is enough for now."

"Maybe it's the soul of my dead grandpa, who had a jinn friend."

"A jinn friend?" The girl laughed for the first time. "Yazidis are Kurds, and Kurds are children of jinn. You are descendants of King Solomon's jinn. I'd expect you all to be brothers and sisters of the jinn, not merely friends!"

Gazing into the girl's glittering purple eyes, Nazo asked, "Did the jinn give you this eye color?"

"It's a mutation called Alexandria Genesis. The legend began a thousand years ago in Egypt when a mysterious light flashed in the sky and everyone who went outside to see it developed pale skin and purple eyes. These individuals came to be known as spirit people. They moved north and eventually disappeared altogether."

"So you got this from your Egyptian ancestors?"

"No. Absolutely not. Probably from my mother's side. She was British." Her voice choked and her purple eyes moistened. "We lost her to cancer last November. That's when Dad started to act like a lunatic." There was a moment of silence, then, as if she remembered something: "The first modern case of Alexandria Genesis was a British woman named Alexandria Augustine from London in 1329."

"Don't tell me you're one of the immortals," Nazo joked.

The girl remained perfectly serious. "Not really, but people with Alexandria Genesis live well over a hundred years. If I can get out of my marriage, I might live to be as old as a hundred seventy."

"That's a lot for the people who live under ISIS."

"I'm not planning to spend it here!" She thought for a moment while eyeing Nazo carefully. "There's more. My vision is twenty-twenty. I never develop any hair apart from what I was born with."

"So you've never had to shave?"

"Yeah." She laughed. "Plus, I have a well-proportioned body. I never gain weight, regardless of what or how much I eat."

"Now that's an advantage." Nazo joined in the laughter.

"Maybe the jinn inside you burns up all the food."

"I'm not possessed by the jinn, as my father thinks. I only communicate with them. Those creatures were created out of the hot desert winds blowing on a smokeless fire. The whirl-winds that carry the dust turn into spinning pillars and cause the swift movement of the jinn. They're skilled in operating time machines. The jinn wander through the lower levels of Heaven and eavesdrop on the angels, then they confide the news to trusted humans."

"I hope I can be trusted too," said Nazo.

"I'm sure you will be. By the way, I'm Mirvat." She stretched out her hand.

Nazo's fingers trembled slightly as she accepted Mirvat's handshake. "You know, if you have a comb or brush, I can calm that wild tangle on your head."

Amusement lit Mirvat's face with the charm of youth's beauty. "Would you? I've back-brushed it like mad, and I'm afraid I'm too impatient to comb it out without breaking it all off. And . . ." The girl's face fell as she suppressed a tiny sniffle. "And it'd be like hangin' with my friends in Dover."

"Dover?"

"In Britain, like the White Cliffs of Dover, just across the channel from France."

"Is that where you're from?"

The girl nodded, handing Nazo a fine-toothed comb. In silence, Nazo started working from the ends.

When Nazo moved from the side she'd completed to the side that remained tangled, Mirvat groused, "If I could get to a store, I'd so snag a pack of gum! This place sucks. I can't do anything without Dad accompanying me, and he's too busy trying to start Armageddon to even notice me. I think he's trying to marry me off so he doesn't have to bother with me anymore."

Nazo didn't know what to say to that, so she just nodded.

"I don't belong here, dammit! I belong back in Dover, running with my girls. They're practically my sisters, ya know?"

"I think so," Nazo said as she tugged the comb free from a particularly nasty tangle. "What on earth were you doing to your hair?"

"I had it a full eight inches tall." The girl shrugged. "There's nothing better to do. I've secretly listened to everything on my iPod a million times already." She made a gagging noise and rolled her eyes.

Though she had an odd accent and foreign mannerisms, Nazo decided she actually enjoyed working for Mirvat. The girl had an inspiring level of spunk that Nazo respected.

* * *

One afternoon a few weeks later, Mirvat's father came home with a cleric, a jinn exorcist. He turned to the Muslim cleric with a dire frown. "This evil thing must get out of her today!"

The cleric nodded. "*Inshallah.* Otherwise, she will be unfit to wed."

The man bellowed for Nazo to have Mirvat slip into her niqab and be ready for the *jalessa*, the exorcism. Behind Nazo, both men climbed the stairs. In moments, Nazo and Mirvat were sitting on her foam mattress, fully covered with niqabs. They both stood as the two men approached. Then Nazo hurried to the door.

The father grabbed her arm and held firm. "No, stay. We might need you to hold Mirvat during the session."

Uneasy, Nazo watched Mirvat sit, then stand, and then sit again in rapid sequence.

The cleric put his hand on Mirvat's head, who sat shaking under the niqab. "My daughter, first, I call upon you to clear and purify your heart. There should not be any evil, disbelief, hypocrisy, or falsity. I, therefore clean the heart first so that when the verses of treatment are read, they meet a pure heart. Otherwise, the verses will meet a defiled, sick heart not capable of treatment."

Mirvat nodded.

"What is your name?"

"Mirvat."

The cleric began reciting some verses, then asked again, "What is your name?"

"Sohrab," said a masculine voice through Mirvat.

"What nationality are you?" The cleric addressed the jinn as if he'd performed the *jalessa* frequently.

"I am Pashtun from Afghanistan."

"Fear Allah. Promise Allah the Almighty that you'll leave this girl and protect her from the others of your kind. Swear by Allah, the One who split the sea for Moses and made the winds blow for Solomon: I will leave her and never return again."

"I will not leave her! I love this girl; I met her when I was on a mission to the UK."

"I'll read more verses of the Holy Quran over her until you flee."

"I am a Muslim jinn. I love listening to the Holy Quran."

The cleric scowled as he lost his patience. "Then I'll drive you out with a severe beating!"

He signaled for Nazo and the father to hold her feet tightly and took a stick from under his cloak. He started by flogging her feet, leaving thin, raw strips across the soles. Then he moved to hit her on her neck and shoulders.

Mirvat's screams grew louder as he continued beating, then the male voice yelled, trembling with great pain, "I'm leaving! I'm leaving!" Mirvat fainted on the foam mattress.

Panting over her, the cleric broke into a broad, victorious smile. He continued to utter his treatment, quite pleased with his progress.

Disappointed that she wouldn't be able to speak further to the jinn about her baby, Nazo hurried from the room, her feet aching in terrorized empathy. That evening, brown eyes rimmed with tears met Nazo after she had completed her chores.

"Damn, when will this insanity end? I hate this war, and I hate this place! Every night from my window, I watch men planting dead bodies in the farmland all around," said Mirvat, her ruddy face almost cinnamon-red in anger, her words pronounced with more venom than Nazo had ever dared. "You know," eyes brimming with rage, she growled to the closed door, "I miss Mom too. You can't just throw me away because I remind you of her." A fat, angry tear trailed down the girl's cheek.

Concerned, Nazo pressed her finger to her lips in an attempt to shush the foolish girl.

"Don't *shh* me!" she growled. "I'm s'posed to wed an ISIS fighter, be some great virgin reward for his service to the cause like all the girls who had their families and joined while their heads were still in bubblegum la-la land."

"Pity, you know, when you're young, you tend to grab the bull by the horns, and you get gored," said Nazo.

"I'm not interested in bullfighting." She laughed. "I wanna see the world, feel the sun and wind on my skin!"

Nazo had no idea of how to help her. "Perhaps you can summon the jinn back and get some guidance?"

"You don't get it. I—" She shook her head, exuding misery. "First, they'd just beat me worse, but I—" The girl dabbed her eyes with her sleeve. "I was faking."

"What! But your eyes!" Nazo gasped.

"Contacts. I ordered them off the net before we left, figuring I might have some use for them." The teen's sly smile reappeared. "Oh, I didn't think I'd use them for *this* insanity. I just thought playing at Alexandria's Genesis would be a bit of fun in this hellhole. It never occurred to me I'd be locked in a room until that man could sell me to the highest bidder."

"So—?" Nazo knit her brows. "So, it was all a lie?"

"One of my best, though I never expected it to end like that . . ." Massaging both feet, she let out a little snort that turned into a mischievous chuckle. "Alexandria's Genesis came from a stupid fanfic, which that man I'll never call Dad again would know if he ever had a second to spare for me."

"But what about my pregnancy and the shaking tray?"

"I bounced the table with my knee, and you're starting to show."

Nazo stifled a giggle, but the next thing she knew, she and the girl were roaring with laughter.

Every morning, Nazo attended to her chores as usual, but some unease floated on the air about the men who ate their breakfast in near silence. She completed the minimal cleaning and hurried upstairs with Mirvat's breakfast.

"I won't be here tomorrow," Mirvat muttered one morning, as she sat up, eager for her tea and toast with marmalade. "You and me, Nazo, we're getting the hell outta of here. No way am I gonna be some twisted trophy bride. I'll be at the embassy in Ankara before my ol' man can say scat. I'll be back in Dover by my birthday, have a nice celebration with my friends."

Nazo blanched. "How will the Turks treat a Yazidi Kurd like me? And the Brits won't process my refugee papers for months . . . if at all."

"True," Mirvat admitted before chewing in thought. "So where do you want to be?"

"Mount Shingal. If my Azad is alive, that's where he'll be."

"Ooh la-la, Nazo has a boyfriend," the girl teased. "I bet he's some hunky, blue-eyed Yazidi man with powerful arms and soft lips."

Nazo could feel the heat rush to her cheeks. "He does have blue eyes," she admitted.

"So, girl, tell me everything."

* * *

After breakfast the next morning, one of the armed guards escorted Nazo to the neighborhood market to buy supplies for the house. She thought she'd found everything Mirvat had requested. On the tray with the girl's dinner was a bucket of ice and a bottle of alcohol, but the sleeping pills lay tucked away in secret.

"What's all this?" asked the father gruffly.

"She needs ice for pain and alcohol to keep her wounds clean," Nazo stated, since Mirvat had been whipped for impudence the day before.

"Carry on then," he growled. Before he turned to walk away, he sighed heavily and put his hand to his temple as if his head ached.

Nazo mounted the stairs and opened the door. Inside, Mirvat had her hair pulled into the tightest ponytail Nazo had ever seen. The tail bounced as the girl padded forward. "Do you have them?"

Nazo pulled out a pack of sleeping pills from under her long dress.

"Oh, girl! You did it!" She kissed Nazo on the cheek "You're a doll."

"I hope it will help you to get some sleep now instead of staring at the walls all night," said Nazo.

"I have things on my mind."

"I hope none of those things involve another jinn." Nazo laughed.

"Not unless you want to summon the cleric again." She fell silent for a moment. "Nazo, the pills are for you."

"Oh. I have many things on my mind—it's true—but I have learned to sleep with them now."

"Listen, tomorrow afternoon, my old man delivers the money to the big boss. He'll be gone for two days. I need you to crush the whole pack of sleeping pills into the guards' dinner. I have arranged everything. Two sets of niqabs. I even nicked some cash from the till last night." She shrugged. "The old man blamed the transporters who brought the money."

"Let them rot in Hell, filthy animals."

"Are you in, Nazo?" Mirvat stretched out her hand and offered Nazo the small box.

"It'll be the best meal they'll ever have."

Late the next morning, the father left for his monthly trip escorted by two Humvees. That meant two days for Mirvat to reach the border and disappear among the refugees crossing into Turkey and two days for Nazo to reach the Kurdish territories in Kobani. The girls skipped around Mirvat's room as the caravan left the property, though Mirvat grunted in pain on each landing.

Later Nazo prepared rice and local yogurt for the guards' lunch. She crushed the whole pack of sleeping pills into the yogurt and added some extra mint, cucumber slices, and garlic to cover the bitterness. Then she served the lunch to the two guards and hurried to Mirvat's room.

An hour later they donned their new loose *abayas* and gloves, then covered their heads with double-layered black veils. Mirvat handed over a stack of bills to Nazo and hid the rest somewhere under her layers.

The two girls then tiptoed down the stairs. As they passed by the living room, they saw the two guards lying on sofas, snoring in deep slumber. They locked the door against the guards and hurried into the street.

After a five-minute walk, they arrived at the main street and waved to a taxi driver. "The National Hospital, brother," said Mirvat. "This pregnant woman needs urgent medical assistance, and our *mahram* are on a Jihadi mission."

"Get in, sisters. I shall be your *mahram* and act as an older brother for you," said the driver.

The taxi roared to the hospital, but once he was paid, the driver lost all interest in his sisters. At the hospital gate, Nazo and Mirvat gazed at each other through their veils. Both nodded and walked away in different directions.

Nazo wandered through the old bazaar thinking of her next step. Should she stop another taxi or walk into the alley and knock at a door? Her pondering stopped with the harsh voice of a *hezbah* policeman.

"Hey, woman," he repeated, "why are you walking around without any male family member?"

Nazo froze in place. "I was in the hospital," she said in a broken Iraqi Arabic accent.

The policeman looked her over. "You shall accompany me to the *hezbah* headquarters and will be released once your husband or brother shows up and pays your fine." He herded Nazo to the police truck and asked the driver to take off.

At the *hezbah* headquarters, a sergeant asked Nazo for contact information for her family so they could summon a man to get her.

Nazo put her head down, gazed at the concrete floor, and switched to an Iraqi Mosul accent. "I'm from Mosul and married to a *mujahed* from Dayrzoor, but he's now on a fighting mission, and I don't know anyone else in this city."

The *hezbah* officer asked Nazo to lift her double-layered veil.

Nazo knew she was caught.

Once she lifted it, the officer glared at her. "Shame on you, filthy liar. Your mother failed to raise you as a decent woman. Did you think we would buy such a story? You are a runaway Yazidi *sabiya*! Who is your owner?"

Nazo's heart broke as she realized she might never see her mother again, never be absolved for sneaking off to see Azad. But the thought that she carried his baby lent Nazo strength enough to put words on her lips. The truth, in this moment, certainly wouldn't set Nazo free. Nazo issued a silent prayer as she said, "My owner was a Libyan from Dayrzoor and was martyred in battle."

"God bless his soul." The officer nodded. "Now you are property of the state then. You will be held in jail till your case is decided."

While fighting back her emotions so they couldn't overwhelm her, Nazo was hustled outside. After a half-hour drive, the police truck arrived at the women's prison, a half-destroyed, two-story building in the southern suburbs of Raqqa. Following the registration and the body search that left her again penniless, a *hezbah* policewoman pushed Nazo along a corridor, then down the stairs to a dim cell.

After the policewoman locked the iron-bar door, Nazo lifted her veil to look around.

A girl rushed to Nazo. "Are you a Yazidi?"

Nazo nodded.

"I'm Jihan from Talezir Village." She threw her arms around Nazo and wept.

Tears welled in Nazo's eyes but refused to fall. She collapsed on one of the four rusty iron beds.

In the afternoon, after they ate the only meal they'd be given that day, the *hezbah* officer shoved another woman into the cell.

Jihan ran to the crying woman. With a protective hug, she helped the woman to the bed, where she continued her sobs.

"This is Caroline, an American held hostage by the Daesh. They come often and take her for a few days, but then return her to the cell," Jihan whispered.

"Why is that?" Nazo asked.

"It's another story. . . . I'll tell you later."

* * *

In the evening, Caroline woke from her sleep, greeted by the smiling faces of the two women. "We have a new resident in the hotel?"

"Actually two. She's carrying a baby!" said Jihan.

Caroline stood up and gave Nazo a warm hug. "Welcome to the hotel. I hope we become great friends."

"Is there any chance that we can check out of this hotel?" asked Nazo.

"I'm afraid this is the Hotel California. 'They can check you out anytime they like, but you can never leave,'" Caroline mumbled in tune. "Have you heard of the song?"

The girls shook their heads. "We must find an exit, though," said Jihan.

Nazo grinned. "I'm in."

Caroline fought back tears. "You go ahead with your plans. I think with my foreign looks I'd only make your journey harder, but I'll keep my fingers crossed for you."

Jihan picked up a piece of paper and pen from Caroline's bed, wrote a phone number, and gave it to Nazo. "Memorize this number, then destroy the paper. A Yazidi girl who was here earlier gave it to me. Contact it whenever you have the chance to get out of here. It belongs to a fellow Yazidi, a man from Iraqi Kurdistan called Pseudo Abu Peling. He runs an underground network to help captured Yazidi girls to return to their families. You just call him, and he'll send his men to pick you up anywhere in Syria or Iraq."

* * *

Almost two weeks later, Caroline's face paled as she heard the sound of the cell door. Two *hezbah* policemen came down the stairs, grabbed Nazo and Jihan by the arms, and pulled them up the stairs.

Once they were in the sergeant's office, Nazo saw a short man with long, curly hair dressed in white Afghan-style baggy trousers and a loose shirt. The officer turned to the man. "These are your *sabiyas*." To the girls, he added, "You were property of the state, and now both of you are sold to our brother."

The girls nodded in obedience, thrilled to be out. Nazo asked the officer, "Sir, can we say goodbye to Caroline?"

"No." The officer's face flashed with heat. He leaned back in his chair. "*Mashallah*, how soon you become friends!" He then turned to their new owner and huffed, "See how these infidels support each other?"

OVER THE next few days, the YPG, People's Protection Units from Rojava carved a secure corridor of dirt trails through the area controlled by ISIS. Many people on the mountainside took this opportunity to cross into the Kurdish territory in Syria. Omed and Soz joined the thousands of displaced people on the trek to safety. Around them, some of the children descended the mountain barefoot, while others walked in worn-out shoes. Yet everyone smiled despite the pain of swollen feet and lips cracked from dehydration and heat.

At the bottom of the mountain, the refugees reached the newly made dirt trail across the field. Soz helped Omed climb onto one of the trucks waiting for them along the road.

Packed with people, the truck drove down the bumpy road, a plume of dust trailing behind. It swirled everywhere, landing on people's faces and in their hair. Children squeezed their eyes shut while their bodies bounced on the hard floor of the truck.

Kurdish fighters stood on alert at either side of the road, hiding behind newly dug earthen mounds to fend off ISIS fighters who roamed the nearby villages. As the truck sank in the shifting sands of the desert, gunfire from a Dushka machine gun burst from a mudbrick hut on the outskirts of an Arabian village about a half-mile south of the road. The YPG patrol fighters shot back from their own Dushka mounted on the bed of their truck. As they streamed through the crossfire, a woman at the rear of Omed and Soz's truck screamed.

"Help, she's in labor!" shouted another woman.

Weary but dutiful, Soz pushed her way through the crowd until she reached the woman. Four women lifted a blanket over the one in labor to provide some privacy as the truck continued to bounce. Beads of dusty sweat ran down Soz's forehead while she checked the woman's racing pulse. Some children poked their heads under the blanket to get a peek, but the encircling women pushed them back. Filled with worry over the baby's fate, Soz kneeled between the woman's legs and urged her to push.

The woman must have been in labor for a while already, because after only a few minutes, the primal scream of a newborn girl silenced the Dushkas on both sides. Soz cut the umbilical cord with the bayonet tied to her waistband. Still on her knees, Soz raised the baby, the newborn life, in her bloody hands and gave the newest soul to her mother. The woman laid the baby on her lap and wrapped her child in her white headscarf.

As Soz tended her, the baby girl's mother wept. She wailed that she'd lost her husband a few days back defending the Shrine of Sharafadin against an ISIS effort to demolish the *Mazar*—mausoleum. She wanted, needed, her husband with her in this moment as the girl was her first child, and now would be their only child.

A YPG patrol vehicle overtook their truck, and the children waved a V-sign to the fighters, who played a cheery Kurdish anthem at full blast. Then the truck arrived at the berm of sand that marked the border with Syria.

Soz gazed at the US Army Humvees pointed at the hostile desert surrounding them. "Even these Humvees have their own story to tell." She turned to Omed. "These Humvees belonged to the US Army deployed in Iraq. Once the Americans left Iraq, they gave them to the newly formed Iraqi Army who abandoned them as ISIS marched on the city of Mosul. Then ISIS moved these Humvees to Raqqa, their Syrian capital. Now the Kurdish fighters have captured them from ISIS during their recent clashes. God only knows where they will head next."

Omed thought for a moment. His mind obviously elsewhere, he commented, "I hope our Yazidi girls captured by ISIS will also one day return to their homes."

Soz could do nothing but nod.

* * *

Omed watched Soz jump off to chat with the YPG fighters gathered behind a berm of hard brown soil. She asked for a smoke as the truck eased across the border and then climbed back on board. From the Iraqi side, more trucks loaded with Yazidi refugees streamed through the clouds of dust. Young Kurdish volunteers from the border villages on the Syrian side threw cartons of bottled water and biscuits into the passing trucks.

Hopeful, Omed leaned over the tailgate and placed his fingers in a V-sign horizontally across his lips. When he caught the eye of one of the volunteers, the young man threw a pack of cigarettes to him.

Across the border, Omed and Soz's truck tracked north, toward the Nawroz camp in the Kurdish city of Derik. All around, long columns of trucks brimming with refugees crossed the border into Kurdish-controlled Syria. Some trucks headed northeast and crossed back to the safe towns in Iraqi Kurdistan.

By afternoon, Omed stood at the gate of the Nawroz camp and watched the tattered tents fluttering wildly in the brisk winds. Hundreds of families dashed ahead in search of any empty tent. Other new arrivals sat in the shade of rocks or slept on blue tarps. The Nawroz camp had been set up originally to shelter the displaced Syrians who'd fled their own civil war, and Omed quickly realized it wasn't equipped to cope with the arrival of tens of thousands of Yazidi families from Iraq.

"Aren't you going to fight for a tent for us?" Omed asked Soz, only half kidding.

"You have to learn how to fight first," Soz replied. Then she ran off with the crowd to secure a tent for the new mother and her child.

Omed walked back to the truck and found a spot where he could rest for the night.

The driver, who would head back for more refugees come morning, opened the toolbox attached to the side of his truck and pulled out his cooking gear. The smell of boiling rice soon filled the air, making Omed realize how long ago his last meal had been. Once the rice was done, the driver nodded to Omed that he had enough to share. He then put some water mixed with tomato paste and white beans into another pot and put it on the stove.

As Omed gratefully consumed his first warm meal in many days, he gazed at the tattoos covering the driver's arms.

"Want one?" asked the driver.

He unbuttoned his reeking shirt. "If I have room for it among . . . my paintings."

"Ah, nice sketches." The driver was indifferent to his sins as he eyed the cuts on Omed's chest that surrounded the bandaged gunshot wound. "Is it the map to a secret treasure?"

"Yes, my soul."

The driver grinned and shook his head sagely. "With all these wars around, we all become kind of psycho."

"Yeah." Omed dropped his eyes to his lap. "The difference between ISIS and us: they hurt others, but we hurt ourselves just to prove we exist."

"I can give you a little more pain so you'll know you're alive," he offered. As Omed took off his shirt, the driver got his tattooing kit from behind the seat. "Want anything in specific?"

"Use your imagination." With that, Omed watched in thoughtful silence as the driver tattooed a razor blade dug into a fake gash over Omed's X-ed-out heart.

Once the driver finished, he held out a piece of broken mirror. "I guess you won't need to cut tonight."

Omed gazed at the tattoo through the dusty sliver of mirror. "Brilliant."

* * *

Soz found a filthy blanket to lay on the floor of the tent. She helped the young woman lie down, then she picked the newborn baby from her mother's arms and laid her inside an empty wooden apple box that she had begged from a truck driver outside.

"We need to get you to the hospital. This is no place for a newborn," she said. "I'll go and arrange for us to be transported to the nearest hospital."

It took a little time for Soz to convince a driver to take them so late in the day, but they soon arrived at the hospital.

When the nurse asked for the baby's name for her birth record, the mother turned to Soz. "You've been so kind. What's your name?"

"Soz."

"Then Soz is your name, my little one." The woman proudly kissed her baby's forehead.

In the morning, Soz returned to the battered tents in a truck loaded with donations from the local community in Derik. Living in utter poverty themselves, the local Syrian Kurds opened their houses and shared their meager supplies with the Yazidi people. Hordes of desperate refugees swarmed the truck as it slowed to hand out the sparse food and water donations.

To the left of the lorry, the driver from the day before was washing his face when Soz came to ask him if he had seen Omed, who was sleeping on a piece of cardboard nearby. She tapped Omed's shoulder to wake him.

A thin layer of dust was caked on his face and body. Soz could not hold back her giggle. Specks of dust fell from his eyebrows into his eyes as he opened them, and more dust fell when he raised his hand to rub his irritated eyes.

"Get up. Let's go to the hospital to dress your wounds and take a shower."

Soz held a plastic jug of water over his head as he struggled to his feet, pouring just enough water to settle the dust. When he shook his wet head, water flew as if he were a soaked dog shaking dry.

He looked at the distant Turkish mountains. "Maybe after the hospital, we'll go to a Turkish bath on the other side of the border." He thought for a moment. "But, to paraphrase Shakespeare, all the perfume of every rose in Damascus won't eliminate the stink from my body, and all the waters of the Tigris won't wash me clean."

"I think Shakespeare meant the stink of blood spilled in evil, not body odor!" She laughed.

"There will be the smell of blood on my hands soon," Omed promised.

"Mine too. They've massacred us for hundreds of years; now they lop off our heads and plant us in the ground. They forgot we have roots. We always grow again, yet we always live at the mercy of others. Nobody will protect us; we must take up arms and defend ourselves."

"I remember what they taught us in school, King Hammurabi's Code; an eye for an eye and a tooth for a tooth."

Soz spat her distaste. "We still suffer from his Mesopotamian curse. Eye for an eye will leave the whole world blind . . .

or without heads." She watched a group of Yazidi children playing with bullet casings near the gate of the camp. "We have to fight ISIS, but we want our children to go to schools."

"ISIS's violence can be contained by weapons, but their ideology can only be changed by books," Omed affirmed.

* * *

Outside the shower in the hospital ward, Soz sneaked a peek at the beads of water glistening on Omed's naked shoulder as she handed him some clothes through the curtain. She couldn't take her eyes off him as he entered the tiny treatment room in his new green military uniform with a flag patch of a red star on a yellow field affixed to the upper left of his chest.

She finally admitted to herself that he was an attractive and kind man, both strong and honest. He made her laugh. Omed was the kind of man who would work to the bone to make a home with her, a man who wanted deep roots. As Omed lay on the treatment table, she asked herself for the first time what she wanted in life.

Soz forced her mind back onto her work. She cleansed his leg wound with some antiseptic and applied fresh bandages. Then she asked him to take off his shirt.

She gazed at the new razor tattoo on his X-ed-out heart. "It seems you had great fun with the truck drivers last night!"

"Yeah, they were awesome. They've traveled many roads. Discovered many places. They face harsh weather; they run into all the crazies, people like me and some ISIS fighters yesterday. They had great stories to tell, the essence of a real life."

"You forgot the part when they pick up women along the road."

"A story without a woman is like food without spice," Omed added with a grin.

"If I had to be a spice, I'd be a hot pepper."

Omed's grin widened. "You're already hot!"

They both laughed. They walked from the hospital to the YBS military training camp. Groups of Yazidi refugees had joined the camp so they could go back to Iraq and drive ISIS from the Mount Shingal region. Again, Omed watched Soz walk away, headed for the nearby training camp for YBS women. Omed entered the men's camp, where men young and old jogged on a two-hundred-yard concrete road along the compound wall. Even in the sweltering triple-digit heat, they broke into occasional sprints, push-ups, stretches, and lunges.

Recognizing an officer's insignia, Omed came forward and introduced himself to a drill sergeant, a man Omed soon realized Soz had spoken of highly. The sergeant took in Omed's injuries and, much to his relief, decided he would only attend lectures on guerrilla tactics and learn how to handle the rifles and rocket-propelled grenades.

In no time, Omed walked across the yard with an AK-47 slung across his shoulder and a relic of a bayonet tied to his cartridge belt. His first lesson was how to dismantle and reassemble his rifle blindfolded, so he could do so in the dead of night on the battlefield.

* * *

As the stars paled and the sun peeked over the horizon, Soz joined the other women in their morning drills and chanted, "Shingal, we will be back soon! Partridges will sing again! Narcissus will bloom again!"

The rest of the morning was spent learning about rifles. The instructor repeated, "Your AK-47 should always be handy and loaded. It should be the closest thing to you at all times. Take care of it so it will take care of you, like your boyfriends. Name your rifle after someone dear to you."

The women giggled as they thought of names. Soz found herself stuck between two names: Soleen, her beloved sister, or Omed, the charming psycho. Somehow, the latter seemed more appropriate.

After fifteen days of combat and physical training, Soz and Omed were ready for their first group dance circle. Taking his hand, Soz danced shoulder to shoulder with Omed as the music grew louder. As they bounced together, young and strong and hopeful, her long black hair flew, occasionally whipping into his face.

After their dance, the YBS leader asked her to come forward. Soz beamed with pride when he announced that she would head the newly formed combat unit of Yazidi men and women who had all lost their families to ISIS. The elated unit members hugged their drill officers and the other trainees from different parts of Syria.

Then, as her first official act, Soz ordered her unit to climb into the two pickup trucks that the YBS had assigned to their unit. When she pointed toward Mount Shingal, the trucks leaped forward, everyone eager to cross over the border and join the fight for freedom.

Yet as they passed by a group of newly dug graves at the foot of Mount Shingal, one of the trucks pulled to a stop. Soz signaled for her own to stop and hopped out.

In a voice full of gravel and thorns, Rezan, one of Soz's fiercest fighters, asked Soz to help her cut the long braid that dangled down her back. Soz took her sharp-edged bayonet and cut through the woman's hair.

As Soz handed her the braid, a tear dropped from Rezan's eye. "Will you walk with me?"

In answer, Soz merely draped a protective arm across the woman's shoulders and walked beside her.

The two women climbed the hillside and walked among the long lines of graves decorated with bunches of flowers. Rezan stopped by one of the graves and hung the braid on the gravestone. "This is my martyred husband. He was killed in a fight with ISIS three weeks ago." Rezan's tears flowed freely.

Soz, remembering her own slaughtered family, hugged her tightly, and they sat by the gravestone to weep. It was very comforting to share a good crying session. After a few moments, however, Soz said, "The tears in our eyes will not bring back our loved ones or drive ISIS from our homes. Let our blood boil in our veins so our unfallen tears evaporate. Let ISIS see nothing but the fire in our eyes as we face them!" She helped Rezan to her feet.

As they descended the hill, Soz wiped a handful of water from her bottle down her face. She might have let Omed witness her grief, but she didn't want the other members of her unit to know that she'd cried over the dead.

* * *

A few days later, her unit had completed the preparations for their first combat mission. Before they set off, the women sat and helped each other braid their hair, except for Rezan who gazed at her wedding photos on her phone.

They set an ambush for ISIS patrols near one of the Yazidi villages. Soz watched through her binoculars, and only half an hour later, a truck loaded with ISIS fighters left the village. She watched it approach, both eager and repulsed. Once the truck's front tire reached a specific stone in the road, everyone opened fire.

One of her unit members launched an RPJ-7 rocket. Everyone cheered as the rocket hit the middle truck sending the wounded ISIS fighters tumbling through the air.

With the fighters stunned or dying, the unit raided the truck from both sides while Soz ran after the only ISIS fighter who escaped. He was inside her range, but she wanted to take him alive. The YBS needed information.

The scrambling ISIS fighter skidded in an effort to evade the bullets he expected but pitched forward, landing face first. His race was lost.

As Omed and other members of her unit dashed up beside her, the ISIS fighter begged for mercy and then for water. Omed helped him to his feet and searched him, then Rezan came forward and gave him some water.

"He's mine," Soz informed her unit. "I'll take care of interrogating him."

Soz directed Rezan to take him off to the side of the road. There Soz asked the terrified man everything the YBS wanted to know. Once she was done with him, Soz leveled her gaze on the nameless ISIS fighter. Beads of sweat dripped from his head into his long, dusty beard. Then Soz stepped back, leaving him to Rezan's tender mercies. She raised her gun and leveled it between his eyes.

Before she pulled the trigger, Omed dashed forward. "Wait, I have a use for him."

Soz nodded her approval with a grim smile.

Omed grasped the ISIS man by his hair and forced him to his knees. He took out his sharp, brand new bayonet. Soz and the others watched in anticipation as Omed started to sing. The tip of his blade danced along to the tune, carving into the ISIS fighter's forehead.

The man screamed from the searing pain but jabbered his gratitude to still have his head. Blood dripped down his nose and landed in plump drops on the ground. After he'd finished his brushstrokes, Omed took out his lighter and lit a cigarette. He then moved the flame along the X he made on the man's forehead. The man let out a piercing cry. Omed leaned back and drew a deep puff on his cigarette as he gazed at his new painting. Behind Soz, everyone moved forward to get a close look at Omed's work. They burst into a gale of cruel laughter as they stared at the carving. Omed helped the ISIS man to his feet. Then he flicked his lighter again, making the fighter wince in fear of renewed pain. Instead, Omed put a cigarette in the man's mouth and lit it for him.

"Now run for your life. You have two minutes before we start hunting you. Tell your masters that the X is courtesy of the Useless Dick. They'll understand," Omed growled in the man's ear.

Free, the ISIS man stumbled as he ran. Moments later Omed fired a couple of shots in the air, then he turned to his fellow fighters. "I'm done. Let's go."

Soz grinned. "You let him go? You're a psycho, you know that?"

"Well, I needed someone to carry my message," Omed replied with a wink as he cleaned the blade of his bayonet.

THE SLAVE dealer herded Nazo and Jihan into a large hall packed with other Yazidi girls brought earlier from Iraq for the auction. From wall to wall, women and girls awaiting their unknown fate wept. ISIS fighters pinched the girls as they walked through the throng, laughing and joking with each other about the girls' charms.

A couple of ISIS fighters approached Nazo. "Yummy, almond brown eyes and an intelligent girl," observed the first fighter, eyeing Nazo's big breasts.

"That! With the penguin walk? Are you blind? She limps."

"Her upper part caught my gaze."

Nazo bit the man's finger as the second fighter approached to check her teeth.

"Oh, you are a little tiger, aren't you?" He laughed, despite the imprint of her teeth in his flesh.

"Come on, this girl's a troublemaker. Let's find something younger," said the first fighter.

Nazo's face froze as she glimpsed Sarah standing in a corner of the hall. She wailed as she ran toward her. Nazo hugged her as tightly as she could and as long as her legs would hold her. Sarah made her strange noise. Her hands were flying in the air, making rapid signs to express the wave of emotions flooding her to be reunited with the only person in the world who understood her.

They both sat on the floor, conversing, unaware of the world around them. Nazo understood that Waleed from Mosul had broken his promise. He had sold Sarah to a slave dealer instead of sending her to the mountain.

A Syrian man, seventy if he was a day, approached the two girls. He gazed at Nazo's face and curves. "Get up and follow me; you will belong to me from now on."

"I will be your obedient servant, sir, but I have a small request," Nazo said in a soft voice.

"I have requests too, so you go first," said the old man.

"This little girl is my sister; she is eleven and a deaf-mute. She has no one else. I want her to live with me."

"Deaf and mute?" exclaimed the old man, eyeing Sarah as if she were useless.

"But she's a very hard worker in the kitchen, sir."

"Two things: will you convert to Islam and will you be my devoted wife?"

"We will do as God wishes for us," Nazo replied.

"Great, then. What I hear, she already believes in Allah and not her Peacock Satan." The old man said that last bit with the mocking tone of one who would have life no other way.

The old man signaled to the two girls to follow him and headed for the ISIS officer sitting at the money table near the door of the hall. He made his payments, and now Nazo and Sarah were his.

Once they were in his house, he told Nazo to sleep in the living room until their wedding, while Sarah must sleep in the kitchen.

Nazo told him in a shaking voice, "I'm still married; my husband is on Mount Shingal."

"It makes no difference. You are my property now; I can do what I want with you." He thought for a moment. "Give me your husband's details. I'll check on him for you." He noted down the information and left the house, as if he were actually doing her such a kindness.

Around midnight, the old man walked into the living room and pressed himself against Nazo. She resisted, saying he had to wait until they were married.

The next afternoon the old man came home with a wide, leering smile. "Nazo, I have good news," he shouted as he entered.

Nazo ran from the kitchen toward him. Pale and catching her breath, she cried, "What is it?"

"Your mother was shot dead in Telafar for spitting in her owner's face. Your Azad was killed before he could make it to the mountain, together with your father. I'm your family now. We can be married anytime!"

Nazo collapsed on the floor, and darkness drank her soul. She woke to the sensation of being cold and wet. The old wretch had doused her with water so she'd wake up. Her eyes filled with tears like a cloud holding rain before some wild storm. Then the waterworks began in earnest. She sobbed like she'd never sobbed before. Pain unlike any she'd known spilled from parts of her heart that she didn't even know existed. With a banshee wail, she pulled out clumps of her hair and slapped her face with both hands. The old man carried her to the bedroom and left the house.

She'd even been denied the chance to console herself by attending their funerals. She would never dance along beside her parents' coffins during the procession to the cemetery, never perform the Yazidi rites for the man she loved. The flute and the *daf*, which were played during the Yazidi funerals, rang loud in Nazo's ears. She felt light on her feet and danced across the room, celebrating the lives now lost to her.

The door opened, and the old man came in with a wedding dress in his hands. He threw it on the bed beside Nazo and informed her that their wedding ceremony would be held that night.

In the evening, clad in her wedding dress, Nazo sat on the bed and wrote a note to Azad.

> *Once I read that lost love is like a bullet. What kills you is not the bullet through your body, but the big space it leaves behind. And Azad, your departure has left a big hole in my heart—it won't heal until we meet again.*

> *I was born with a half-soul. All my life I searched for the person with the missing half, and I found it in you. When we met, my half sailed through your blue eyes, deep down, and merged with yours for eternity.*

Now death has separated us into separate realms of the universe. Yet I am also dead—I only need to cremate my body to set my soul free. I don't want to breathe in the world when you are not in it anymore.

Tonight, I will be your bride. Tonight, I will dance with you under the blue raindrops of Heaven.

* * *

After the farce of a marriage ceremony, Nazo walked in her white gown toward the bathroom door, the fingers of her right hand securely clutching the handle of a jerry can of kerosene. Once she was inside the narrow room, she locked the door. Warm black tears of kohl streaked her cheeks as she leaned back against the cold wall. She bent down and raised the heavy jerry can over her head. She lifted her face toward it as she poured every last bubble of anguish over herself until she was soaked. The kerosene washed away the multiple layers of caked-on makeup, leaving her face pale and sheer.

Outside the room, she heard the chanted celebration of the armed men. She closed her eyes and released a sigh. With focused determination, she struck the matchstick against the box. Instantly, its flame surged upward as she opened her eyes. She was eager to set aflame every inch of her dead body. While the last few months of her life flashed before her eyes, she brought the flame close to her face, ready for her immolation.

Before the fire made contact with the hair on her head, she felt something magical—a sensation—a motion inside her womb. Her eyes fixed on the glowing flame, and her ears remained on alert. Rolling waves stroked her from inside, like having a little fish swimming inside her! Another life moved within her!

The matchstick fell from her hand to the floor, extinguished in a puddle of kerosene before the gasses could grow hot enough to burn.

A random collection of happy and sinister thoughts invaded her head. As the thoughts clashed against each other, she collapsed in futility. The rage within her subsided, and she swallowed the sorrows stuck in her throat. She must nurse the wounds to her soul and cling to the thin thread of her life for the sake of the little life inside her. She must wear her pain like rosary beads around her neck. As in the legend of the Phoenix, from the smoldering embers of the person she used to be, she must rise and spread her flaming wings.

She knew her life had come apart as she lost herself in bits and pieces to the circling vultures. Winter had wrapped its freezing arms around her soul. She must weave her torn parts back together as best she could. Her heart might resemble a patchwork quilt, but it could still make a warm home for her child.

A harsh pain gnawed at her insides to remind her that Azad's soul had ascended to the Qappia Asmani—the Gate of Heaven. Nazo knew by now that Azad's soul had crossed the Bridge of Sirat and been judged by Sheikh Adi, the last avatar of Ta'us Malik. Being a sinner like herself, Azad's soul would not have reached the eternal Heaven. His soul had to change its garment. It would soon return to Earth and transmigrate into the material body of a human or animal, to be reborn and continue its education and purification. She implored that the next material body for Azad be the little soul moving within her now.

A heavy knock on the bathroom door disrupted the silent battle inside her head.

"Woman, you must proceed to the bride's room. The groom will be attending soon," yelled the ISIS woman.

Moments later Nazo hurried to the bride's room and locked the door behind her. As she collapsed on the bed, the smell of kerosene filled the room. A dizzy-looking cockroach crawled near the disheveled bed, which desperately needed attention.

When she heard a rattling cough outside her door, Nazo jumped out of the bed and pulled on some fresh clothes. She unlocked the door and leaned into the nearest corner of the room.

When the door cracked open, the ancient groom, clad in a white quilt and a black cloak, stood amid the traditional dancers formed in two opposing lines by the armed ISIS men. His knees threatened to collapse under his body weight; his head trembled slightly under his checkered Arab headdress. Little beads of sweat ran down his sunken cheeks as he peered through the door.

Once the groom was in the room, he wrinkled his nose, probably a protest against the strong scent of kerosene. He stepped on the cockroach as he stumbled over to the bed. He sat on the edge and lit a cigarette, then turned his head to Nazo who remained scrunched into the farthest corner.

"Come to bed," he snarled.

Nazo remained silent but glared at him with true hate.

He rose, towering over her, then grabbed her wrists and yanked her toward him. Nazo extended her leg and kicked his chest, sending him sprawling on his back.

From the fury in his eyes, she knew her rejection was boiling the blood in his veins. The groom ran to the bathroom and came back with a thick rubber hose. He ripped at Nazo's dress as he hit her hard across her body and head. She screamed at the top of her lungs, a loud and ceaseless assault on the senses. She curled into a small ball to avoid the kicks to her belly.

The groom left after he had spent all his frustration on Nazo's body. She lay bruised from head to toe. Several of the blows had landed on her face, and her nose bled.

A while later, Sarah ran to Nazo's room, pale and fear-stricken as blood trailed down between her legs across the concrete floor behind her. Nazo jumped and took her in her arms. Sarah's silent screams echoed in Nazo's ears.

Nazo realized her mistake now. After her rejection, the old man had gone to the kitchen. Sarah told Nazo that he put his hand over her mouth and shoved his other hand up her dress and ripped off her underwear. She hadn't understood what was happening. She didn't know what the rape was. She'd thought it was another nightmare like those that had haunted her sleep after her brother's murder, until the burn between her legs and the fresh stains on the bed told her it had truly happened. Nazo and Sarah sat on the floor leaning their backs against the cupboard. Nazo gazed at the bathroom door, and voices in her head urged her to walk into the bathroom and finish what she'd started. Then she remembered her mother's words when, as a girl, she'd asked her why women put henna on their hair.

"We dye our hair many colors to disguise our gray souls. My daughter, we don't mature by merely growing old but by the damage time causes in our lives. When there are holes in our hearts, scars on our souls, and patches on our wings, then we know we have grown."

Her mother's words lent her strength. She realized that feeling pain was far better than feeling nothing at all. Pain gave her a sense of existence. These hard experiences in her life would hammer her into shape while she was still warm and soft, then turn her heart into cold iron. All these bitter lessons had purpose: to awaken her inner power, to show her the truth about herself and her life's journey.

She sat and plotted her revenge for the attack on Sarah.

* * *

Next morning the old man came home and demanded his breakfast. He avoided looking directly at Nazo's bruised face when he added, "And if you don't fulfill your wifely duties this morning, I will sell your *habibty* sister this very afternoon."

Nazo nodded, avoiding any eye contact as well. "Take a shower. I will prepare your breakfast, then wait for you in the bedroom." As she spoke, Nazo noticed a pack of pills visible through the pocket of his thin white dishdasha, and her mind whirled.

The old Arab whistled and mumbled a folk song as he showered. Nazo stood at the bathroom door and gave him a clean set of dishdasha. As her groom left for the bedroom, she hurried into the bathroom and searched the pockets of his dirty tunic. She snatched the pack of pills and ran back to the kitchen. Viagra. She snorted as she read the package.

She powdered the remaining nineteen blue pills into her husband's homemade yogurt, which she added to his tray with some mint and garlic. Then she sighed as she asked Sarah not to leave the kitchen until she returned.

Smiling, she served her husband a loaf of bread, his yogurt, and a small cup of tea; the first and hopefully last breakfast-in-bed she would serve to her groom.

He ordered Nazo to sit and join him for breakfast. His eyebrows rose in his forehead and his eyes widened when Nazo told him she had to take a shower. She promised sweetly to join him in bed afterward. She ran to the bathroom and turned on the water tap, then hurried to the kitchen and locked the door behind her.

Twenty minutes later, her groom shouted for help. "My head is about to explode, and everything's blurry!"

The moment Nazo entered the room, the groom's eyes rolled back in his head, and he collapsed on the floor in a convulsion. She rolled him onto his back. One side of his face drooped, and then both sides went utterly slack. Her groom was a lifeless body while his penis stood fully erect under the white cotton dishdasha like the center-pole of a Bedouin tent.

Nazo ran back to the kitchen, where both she and Sarah donned niqabs. They held each other's hands. "O, Ta'us Malik, take us under your wings and protect us from the black crows. Guide us with your spirit to safety," prayed Nazo. Then she ran back to the corpse for the mobile phone from his pocket, and they rushed out of the house.

She flew from her marriage home with new dreams, one kicking in her belly and another clinging to her hand. Like the shooting stars, she was wrecked, broken to pieces, but she intended to shine brightly as she fell. Her Arabic-language teacher had told her once when Nazo had dropped her classes, "Don't give up. An Arabian warrior once said, if one has to fall eventually, let it be from horseback."

When Nazo and Sarah were on the street, she took her deceased husband's mobile phone from her bag and dialed the number Jihan had her memorize in the prison. The phone rang, but no one picked up, so she redialed.

"Hello?" asked a man's voice.

"Is this Abu Peling?" Nazo whispered.

"Speaking. How can I help you?"

"I'm a Yazidi girl with my little sister in Raqqa. I need to get to Kobani."

"Give me details about your home address and your owner."

"We're on the run. We've already left the house."

"Ah, good, then tell me exactly where you are now."

"Let me see." She looked across the street. "There's a sign that reads Al Shami Fast Food."

A moment of silence passed. "Stay there and keep hidden from the eyes of the *hezbah* police, and I'll get back to you as soon as possible with details."

Nazo's heart pounded in her ears as her gaze shifted back and forth from her mobile phone to the street, searching for policemen. A few minutes later, her phone rang.

"In fifteen minutes," the same voice said, "a taxi will pull over opposite the restaurant. Its number is 419107. Ask the driver, 'Can you take us north?' When he answers, 'Only if you have a brave heart,' get in the taxi."

Twenty minutes later, a taxi parked across from the restaurant. Nazo took Sarah's hand and approached the driver. "Sir, can you take us north?"

The middle-aged man smiled. "Well, only if you have a brave heart."

The two women scrambled in, and the taxi roared off toward the northern suburbs. Once they arrived in the rural areas, the taxi pulled over. Sarah grabbed Nazo's hand firmly as her hands fluttered about the last time Nazo had left her in a taxi. Nazo gestured to her that she would never leave her alone again.

The driver turned his head to Nazo and told her they had to wait for a second pick-up. He rolled down the window slightly and cautiously smoked while waiting. Finally, a speeding motorbike approached them. A man in a tracksuit and brown headdress pulled over alongside the taxi. He signaled to Nazo and Sarah to get onto the bike. The taxi driver nodded to Nazo, and the two girls got out. Nazo sat on the motorbike behind the driver, and Sarah wedged herself between the two.

* * *

The pale sun disappeared behind floating black clouds as they rode along the rough backroads. Nazo turned her gaze from the moving shadow of the motorbike and leaned forward to make a funny face for Sarah.

As drizzling rain pattered on their heads, she felt the whiz of bullets passing by her ears, and the driver began to zigzag. She fell from the bike on her bad right hip in the shallow mud.

The motorbike continued zigzagging across the desert with Sarah clinging to the driver's waist.

To muffle her screams of pain, she pressed a hand over her mouth and squeezed her eyes shut. She waited for the inevitable sniper shot that would end her life, but it never came.

Creeping along the roadside, she hid in a water-filled ditch. There, she waited for darkness to fall. The cold desert wind whistled in Nazo's ears, and by the time she crawled out her body was shaking with cold. A low, deep cramp made Nazo place her hand on her belly and cry out, but once she felt the baby kicking, her breathing slowed to normal.

She bit her lip to brave the searing pain in her dislocated hip and dragged herself on her left side a few hundred yards toward a faint streak of light glowing in the distance. Heavy mud clung to her torn dress. She collapsed to the ground a hundred feet before she reached the tent's flap. Panting and trembling, she felt the sting of her bruised body.

Then, dragging her right hip, she crept on into the tent. In the light of a faint oil lamp, Nazo spotted the figure of an old woman lying on her back on a mat of woven reeds. Her head nestled on a brick, which she used as a pillow. The old woman writhed in pain on her mat. With rosary beads twisted through her trembling fingers, she murmured her prayers into the night. Lying on her back, Nazo buried her face in her hands and repeated those Sufi prayers until her breath slowed in sleep.

Early in the morning, when Nazo opened her eyes, the old woman was crouched beside her and cleaning the bruises on her body.

In a voice thick with tears, Nazo said, "Salam, Grandma. I ask for sanctuary in your house. Protect me—I have no one but you."

"My daughter, God is the protector," said the old woman as she raised her hands to the sky. The gentleness in this woman's face and voice made Nazo feel comfortable, safe.

A few minutes later, the woman hoisted Nazo to her feet. Propped on the woman's shoulder, she was led to the tiny outdoor reed bathroom. The old woman poured water to bathe Nazo's naked body, and as she did she sang in the sweet tones of a young girl.

When the bath was over, she gave Nazo a black Arabic gown. "I knew you were coming—my wolves told me. I wished you could have arrived during the daytime though, because at night, I can't move."

"Oh, Good Mother, you can communicate with the animals?"

"Love and kindness open the window of the soul. It's a universal language. Once understood, all can speak."

Nazo pulled her black gown over her head. "Good Mother, why are all your clothes black?"

"We wear different clothes, but we're the same inside. Certain colors do make us feel better about ourselves, but they don't necessarily reflect our beings. When we evolve and dissolve into the light of God, then we can see our true colors. Saints don't need to be clad in white, nor the wicked in black." She placed Nazo on the reed mat, put her hand on Nazo's injured right hip, and mumbled a prayer.

In the afternoon, Nazo sat and thought about what could

have happened to Sarah and wept. She had promised never to leave her again! As soon as her hip healed, she would plunge into the desert and find her. She spun through all the possibilities in her mind: being eaten by the desert beasts, dying of thirst, or being returned to ISIS captivity. None of her imagined scenarios included the miracle of survival, but still a hidden power urged her feet toward the endless sand.

The next morning, the old woman woke from her sleep and sat cross-legged. When she noticed the slight limp of Nazo's right leg, she motioned for Nazo to sit beside her. Then her wrinkled hand reached to the edge of the mat and picked up a *daf*.

Nazo's eyes widened. "Oh, my lady, we use the same instrument in our religious ceremonies."

The Sufi woman put her hand on Nazo's right hip. She raised her *daf* and played to the melody that sprung from her soul, praise for the Almighty. Nazo nodded her head to the rhythm of the magical tune that filled the air. Her body felt light, so she joined the Sufi woman as she stood and whirled. Their sonorous, hypnotic voices joined in unison, chanting God's name, each in her own language.

In time with the music, they swung their heads and arms faster from side to side. Their bodies vibrated on the same spiritual frequencies. The Sufi woman, with a cry in her throat, prayed for Nazo to the beat of the drum. An invisible energy carried Nazo from her physical reality into an inner space. She freed her wings and floated across the infinite universe. Her hands moved bubbles of light in the vast space, and her lungs inhaled the cosmic energy. With her soul lost in the ecstasy of the dance, she felt a voice say, "Walk." Nazo steadied herself and stepped with no limp for the first time in her life.

Nazo jumped for joy and threw herself on the Sufi woman. Her eyes filled with tears, Nazo bent to kiss her hand. As she raised her head, her face froze. A pair of gray wolves with large ears and yellow eyes stalked through the half-open tent flap and circled the old woman.

The woman put down her frame drum. She patted one wolf's head before turning to Nazo. "Young girl, you move well."

"You know the Yazidis. We dance with the *daf* on every possible occasion, even our funerals."

The laugh lines on the old woman's face swerved as she curved her mouth to form a smile. Her face was a manuscript, etched deep with her history. The lines told of the days she'd laughed and the days she'd cried. *Why do poets who extol the beauty of youth turn a blind eye to the beauty of the old?* Nazo wondered.

At noon, Nazo went outside to collect some firewood from the surrounding bush to cook some rice. She came back with a pile of dry branches over her head and threw it close to the three-stone stove. When she leaned her head forward into the tent, she stepped back as the pair of gray wolves walked out through the tent flap.

Watching them go, she said, "It seems your guests have left before we could offer them something to eat."

"Don't worry. I offered them some dried meat I kept under my mat."

"Good Mother, how long have you lived here?"

"I have roamed the deserts for quite a long time now."

"You must have seen a lot," Nazo chuckled.

"From every gray hair on my head comes a story, a life experience." She sighed. "But nothing is as magnificent as walking across the desert at night under millions of the twinkling stars and feeling God's eyes watching over you. You feel His breath blowing on your face with every step you take across the shifting sands." She picked up her blue rosary from under her mat and began mumbling her prayers.

"Amen," Nazo said as she picked up the covered cooking pan from the corner of the tent and went outside.

Thirty minutes later, the smell of the boiled rice filled the tent as Nazo carried the pan in. The old woman was still in her prayers. Nazo gazed at the pan with hungry eyes, but she waited for the woman to finish. However, when Nazo offered her a plate, the woman asked to be excused, for she was fasting.

Nazo put the plate aside and sat beside the old lady. "Good Mother, I will fast with you, I have scars on my soul and many holes in my heart."

"Mawlana the Rumi once said that our life's sorrows and pains are like the holes made in the reed flute. So Nazo, my daughter, breathe through your soul, put the tips of your fingers on the holes of your heart, and play the tunes. Only the tunes that come from the holes in your heart can heal the wounds of your soul and make it sing again."

"Can you teach me how to play the *daf*, Good Mother?"

"If you free yourself from all earthly bonds and prepare to unite with God."

"I wish I could see Him." Nazo sighed.

"People call earthly love blind, but the love of God is the light of sight. Love Him and let His light fill you. God is beautiful, and you can see Him in every beautiful thing around you."

Nazo gazed at the *daf* in the old woman's hand and smiled. She stretched her hand and picked it up. Nazo raised the instrument, then breathed from the depth of her soul as her fingers struck the leather skin of the *daf*. She shook her head in time with the rattling of the small chains inside the body of the drum.

As night fell, the woman rolled on her mat and moaned in pain. Her muffled cries pierced Nazo's heart. She sat beside the old woman and rubbed her hands and legs all through the slow night while she listened to the old woman's pleas to the Lord:

> *Deep within my soul dwell the causes of my bereavement and pain. This ailment no medicine can remedy. The sole cure for this pain is the Union with the Friend in Heaven, and by grieving, I hope I will attain what I long for. Death is nothing more than a bridge between friends. The time now nears that I cross that bridge, and friend meets Friend.*
>
> *O, My Beloved God, Another Night is passing away, Another Day is rising—*
>
> *Tell me that I have spent the Night well, so I can be at peace,*
>
> *Or that I have wasted it, so I can mourn for what is lost.*
>
> *I swear that ever since the first day You brought me back to life,*
>
> *The day You became my Friend,*
>
> *I find no comfort in sleeping—*

And even if You drive me from your door,

I swear again that we will never be separated.

Because You dwell in my heart.

O, God, if I worship You

For the fear of Hell, then burn me in Hell.

If I worship You

For the hope of Paradise, deny me the prize.

But if I worship You

For Yourself alone, then grace me with the beauty of Your divine face.

Nazo's lips moved as she listened to the old woman's prayers and watched her tears fall on the blue beads in her hand. They mumbled the prayers and cried until the first light of the dawn crept over the horizon, then Nazo fell into a deep sleep beside her.

A few hours later Nazo woke to the barking of dogs behind the tent. The old woman lay still, unroused but breathing slowly. Nazo jumped from her place as she heard a man calling at the tent door.

Nazo yelled, "Who is that? There are no men in the house, you can't step in!" She paced slowly toward the side of the tent.

"I know. I'm the sheepherder. I've brought some milk and bread for my lady, the Sufi woman."

"Leave it at the door, and I'll pick it up later. God bless you."

Nazo peered through a small hole in the black wool tent and watched the man ride away, with his long legs dangling from the back of a small donkey. It plodded with heavy steps ahead of the cattle while the dogs roamed along the sides of the herd.

Satisfied he was gone, Nazo poured a glass of milk for the Sufi woman, who by now had seated herself on the mat. Before she said anything, Nazo asked her, "How can you live alone, here in the middle of nowhere?"

"I am never alone. He is always with me." The Sufi woman picked up the pitcher and performed ablution for her prayers. After she was done with her prayers, she seated Nazo beside her and told her story.

"Back in the time of those turbulent years in the Arabian desert, I was a young girl caught up in an old world. My mother was a lucky woman. She married my father, a poor man. In fifty years, she never smiled—she had no wrinkles on her face.

"I was the fourth of my sisters. My father was a pious Muslim, who had a small reed raft to help people cross one of the Mesopotamian rivers. When I was born, there was not even a drop of oil in our house with which to anoint the navel of the newborn daughter and no cloth in which to swaddle me. Therefore, my mother told my father to go to our neighbor's house and beg them for some oil so she could light our lamp.

"My father had made a promise never to ask a human being for anything. So he went out and put his hand on the neighbor's door. Without saying anything to them, he returned to our own house. 'They won't open the door,' he said.

"My father and mother both died before I turned ten. A famine swept across the region and separated me from my three sisters. Some thieves kidnapped me and sold me into slavery for six *dirhams*.

"I tried to flee while I was still in the auction, but my owner caught me and broke my wrist. Then I raised my hand. 'Oh, God, I am not asking you to change my fate—I surrender to everything You visit on me—but I ask you to give me the strength to bear my trials and earn your satisfaction.'

"My owner discovered that I had a nice singing voice and could play the *daf*, so he set up a place in the bazaar where I could sing behind a veil. As the days passed, my audience grew larger, and my master forced me to dance as I sang behind the veil to attract an ever-bigger audience.

"When I was about twenty-six, while I prepared myself to sing behind the curtain, all the songs that I used to sing vanished from my memory. Consumed with my fears, I sat on my seat behind the veil. Moments later, I lost control over my tongue and found myself singing from my heart some melody never heard before and lyrics I had never uttered before—all praising God's name and his Kingdom in Heaven. My hands trembled, and sweat flowed down my body. Something had awakened me, and I refused to sing or play for anything except my Beloved God.

"One evening, my angry master came into my room as I knelt for my evening prayers. He sat opposite me, waiting impatiently for me to finish. As I rose from my prayers, an aura of light surrounded me. He jumped from his place. In a choked voice, he told me he'd decided to free me in fear of God.

"I had no place to go, so I headed to the desert for meditation and prayers. Then I led a life of solitude in the mountains, keeping company with the animals that gathered around me every time I played my *daf*. One day, I entered a mosque and sang the poems I'd learned in the mountains.

"As the days passed, I continued to sing in Sufi circles, and my followers multiplied. Men proposed marriage to me and offered me money and gifts, but I declined all the worldly offers that would have distracted me from my union with the Divine Spirit."

Nazo raised her head. "You never fell for a man?"

"All that walk on the dust are dust. I've cut off my heart from the world and curtailed all my desires. My mortal body belongs to this world, but my soul belongs to Him. I have lost my being to Allah. He is the only true Beloved. Ultimately it is through the love of God that we are brought into the unity of Being."

She turned to Nazo. "You know, one day I walked the streets of my town with a torch in one hand and a pitcher of water in the other. When people asked me what I was up to, I shouted, 'I want to set fire to the paradise by this torch and quench the fires of Hell by this pitcher, so both can veil and vanish from the Almighty's kingdom. Only then will the people of faith worship God out of love and not fear or a mere desire to attain a reward.'"

"My Lady, do you follow a specific faith or path to God?"

"For me, the names we give to God and the locations where we worship Him are less important than the purpose for our communion with Him. In my soul, there is a temple—a shrine, a mosque, a church—where I kneel. Prayer should bring us to an altar where no walls or names exist. In my soul, the world dissolves, leaving only God."

Her transgressions beginning in the months since the Daesh arrived in her village filled Nazo's mind. She had given her virginity in love. Deception had become a tool of survival. She had even taken a man's life in cold blood, a horrible man's life but a life nonetheless. "Good Mother, I'm filled with sins," she confessed.

"But you're also filled with love. If you're a lover, then you understand God. And when you understand God, then your sins are naught but drops that will dissolve into the ocean of His Divine Love. Seek God within yourself. Dust off the knowledge buried in your soul. Once it shines, all other inferior desires and emotions will evaporate from the garden of your soul. Some choose to dance with their bodies; others choose to dance with their spirits."

"Can we rid ourselves then from the hate that eats up our bodies and souls?"

"For a true believer, the love of the Merciful God leaves no room for hostility toward other creatures or worldly things. Among the roses, be a rose. Among the thorns, be also a rose."

"Don't you hate evil, like most people do?" Nazo asked.

"I am doused to my ears with the love of God, too much love to care about hating evil." The Sufi saint looked at Nazo. "Let's fast for the coming days so Our Beloved God may turn His mercy on us."

Nazo joined her in prayer, and they both raised their hands to the sky.

* * *

For the following sleepless nights, Nazo prayed with the Sufi woman. In the daytime, she walked the surrounding desert and played the *daf*. One evening, Nazo watched the orange sun sinking into the sands. As the sand glowed red, she played the *daf* that had been a gift from the old Sufi and danced. The winds carried the tune to the horizon while her soul tiptoed into the fallen sun.

When a wolf approached her, her throat tightened and her playing turned to noise. She closed her eyes and resumed her playing while the wolf walked in circles around her. Then she stopped her playing to pat the gray wolf's head. She brought her face closer and gazed into its familiar blue eyes. She felt she could stretch her fingers and touch its soul. Her belly tickled, and a shiver went through her body, as she felt the panting breaths of the wolf on her belly. Nazo remembered Azad and their rendezvous under the fig tree.

When the wolf walked into the darkness, Nazo followed him. They walked the night in silence under the glowing light of the full moon. Then Nazo put her left hand on her belly and sang a Kurdish lullaby as she felt the baby kick. At the early dawn, the wolf stopped at the side of an asphalt road. He raised his head and howled to the fading moon. Nazo cupped the wolf's face—gazed once more at his glittering blue eyes—then leaned forward and placed a kiss on his forehead.

As Nazo walked along the asphalt road, she looked back every few seconds until the blue-eyed wolf had disappeared behind the sands.

Exhausted, Nazo laid herself down on the sand a few yards away from the road and fell asleep. A couple of hours later, she woke to the sound of a truck engine. She hurried to the side of the road and waved for the truck.

The driver, clad in a YPG uniform with an assault rifle slung over his left shoulder, got down from his vehicle and helped Nazo in. As his truck roared down the road, he turned to Nazo and said in Kurdish, "I am Ashti. Welcome, sister, to Rojava, the Kurdish lands of Syria."

Nazo buried her face in her hands and burst into tears.

Once the truck entered Kobani from Shi'rah Hill in the western countryside near the city, Nazo could see from her window the columns of military vehicles packed with Kurdish Peshmerga forces from Iraqi Kurdistan entering the city via Turkey. They came to support their fellow Kurds in Rojava, seeking to drive ISIS out of the remaining pockets in Kobani.

Nazo, with a burning desire, asked the man if they'd received a deaf and mute little girl two weeks back.

The man thought for what seemed an eternity, then smiled. "Yes, she's in the orphanage."

Soon, the truck arrived at the Payman Shelter, a home for children who had lost their parents during the fighting. Nazo hurried in and found Sarah in the corner of the main room, struggling to communicate in her sign language with a female teacher. Sarah dropped her hands and ran to Nazo. She tripped over a school desk and fell to the floor. Nazo lifted her from the ground into her arms and whirled in small circles. Nazo and Sarah would remain there until their border crossing to Turkey could be arranged.

On a chilly December morning, the YPG and Peshmerga fighters launched an offensive to capture Mistanour Hill south of Kobani.

The mission, if successful, would give them control of the ISIS supply routes to Aleppo and Raqqa. Soz's unit had sneaked into Kobani earlier and was ready for the crucial fight.

In the heat of the battle, while their unit charged toward ISIS' fortified positions at the foot of Mistanour Hill, a helpless Omed watched a bullet drill through Soz's high waistband into her belly. Her arms wrapped around her bleeding side, and she stumbled forward a few steps. As she fell to the ground, Omed raced toward her. He lifted her into his arms and carried her to the pickup truck parked behind a three-story building. Then he laid her in the bed of the pickup and rested her head on his lap. He unfastened her thin leather belt, which held two grenades, took off his headscarf, tied it over her wound, and refastened her belt securely.

Though she slipped out of consciousness, Omed talked to her all the way to the hospital. When they arrived, she was taken straight to the operating room. The nurse told Omed that she urgently needed a blood transfusion. Omed waved in their comrades who had followed them in another truck to the hospital. The blood of two volunteers matched with Soz's. The nurse asked one of them, Rezan, to lie on the bed so she could draw a unit.

Though Omed's blood didn't match Soz's, he donated a unit of his blood for the hospital. Afterward, Omed and their other comrades leaned back on the wall of the hallway that led to the operating room and waited. A couple of hours later, Soz rolled out of the ER on a stretcher and headed to the female intensive care unit.

"We have done what we could, and the rest is now in the hands of God," the doctor said in a grim voice devoid of hope.

Omed sat by her bed and held her cold hand. A nurse came in with a plastic bag containing Soz's belongings and handed it over to him. He pulled his bloodstained headscarf out of the bag, buried his face in it, and burst into tears.

He gazed at Soz's face as he rolled up his headscarf and draped it around his neck. Once again, he reached into her bag and picked out Soz's khaki YBS uniform. Patches of dry blood covered the shirt and trailed down her baggy trousers.

Yet a voice in his head urged him to search the pockets. He put his hand in the right pocket of her shirt and found her small mirror and kohl eyeliner. That wasn't what the voice sought. He considered looking at himself in her mirror, but he returned the items to her pocket. He moved to the left breast pocket. His fingers felt a folded leaf of paper and a fresh AK-47 cartridge. The female fighters kept their last bullet for themselves, so the ISIS men never laid their hands on them. He dropped the shirt into the bag, then his fingers trembled slightly as he unfolded the paper. It was a letter written in a feminine hand and soft purple ink:

My beloved,

I'm worried that you will never read this, but I'm happy if it has made its way to your hands. Though that means I'm dead now. By the time you read this, my soul will be floating in another world. But, come on, smile; your name is Omed, which means hope, so never lose it.

I won't go straight to Heaven; believe me. I have piled up a bunch of pretty good sins so that my soul will reincarnate back to this Earth soon. I want you to know that I'll do my utmost to rein-carnate into your future-born daughter so I can be with you the rest of your life. I loved you the moment I laid my eyes on you, and I will love you always. The touch of your smile filled the emptiness in my heart and quenched the flames of my burning soul.

I've used every single move in my body and every word on my lips to shoot you with Cupid's arrows. But they failed to penetrate the thick walls of your heart. I might not be the girl that you see when you close your eyes, but I'm the girl whose world is set on fire by your gaze.

I tried everything to make you see me. I improved my combat skills, became a fierce warrier, and sent a few ISIS men to Hell, but I lost the fight to own your heart. I wanted to kill my feelings before they grew, but I couldn't because my love for you is a part of me now. Even after death, when my body ceases to exist, my soul will scream your name across the infinite universe.

I hated my looks; I only felt beautiful when I was beside you. You looked at my face sometimes, but you were never able to see my heart—maybe because you're still searching for your own. Unappreciated beauty is wasted beauty. It is not beauty which makes us love; it is love which makes us beautiful.

I didn't fall for you because we understood each other. I fell for you because your craziness matched mine. You are everything I wanted in a man, but I wasn't what you wanted in a woman— that didn't change anything, though. I love you, and it is a beautiful thing. I craved the feeling of being loved by someone, which I never had in my life, but that's okay. Know I died happy because I died loving you.

Neither of us had anyone else left to live for, and it burns my heart that you will forever be my friend rather than my husband. Many times, I fantasized about how you would propose to me, about our wedding and our children. I wanted at least a half dozen of them to fill our future home!

Now, I want nothing more than for you to be happy. You are an amazing person. You are also an idiot not to see the flood of emotions that I had dammed inside me.

By "You are an idiot" I mean "I love you," in case you still don't get it, just as you didn't all the other times I tried to say it to you.

Peace,
Soz

Fresh tears welled in Omed's eyes and fell without end. He'd once written a poem so similar. He hadn't known pain until he'd loved someone who didn't love him back. Omed caressed Soz's hair, then knelt down and placed a soft kiss on her forehead.

Women with no conventional beauty were cursed with the plight of ugliness and blessed by its power, spurred on to something greater by the pain of their struggle. While the swarms of hungry flies sought pretty girls soaked in honey all over, other girls hardly attracted anyone, so they clung to the power of their inner beauty. They struggled to mirror their vast interior cosmos into a visual medium, a different beauty to be perceived by the outer world, a struggle Omed knew all too well.

How can I crave to be loved by others when I despise myself?

A realization dawned in his mind suddenly: he'd have to learn to love himself first before he could devote his heart to anyone. The love of the self is the root of a fruitful life, the first major landmark in someone's quest for the elusive thing people called happiness.

He had to find answers to the two questions that whirled in his head: *What are the things that really matter in a woman? What made him think of Nazo while he cried for Soz moments ago?*

He needed to clear his head, and he had the sudden urge to smoke. He went outside the hospital and walked the streets of the burning city. He listened to the shells bursting in the distance while he puffed. The smoke wafted from his mouth, sailed across his vision, and blurred with the clouds of smoke from the bombshells that mushroomed into the sky above Kobani.

He remembered his dream last summer on the roof of his mudbrick house in Shingal. He looked up at the sky and waited for the smoke to clear. The same phoenix with the peacock feathers emerged from a rainbow halo and flew in circles above the hospital—then disappeared into the sun with Soz on its back.

Panicked by his vision, Omed ran back to the hospital, fearing the worst and crying out Soz's name. When a nurse bustled out the door and signaled for him, he hurried behind her to Soz's room.

Upstairs, much to Omed's relief, Soz's eyes fluttered when he entered, panting. Her lips trembled as she raised her hand and felt her nose. "My nose is the same." Hopeless tears welled in her eyes.

"No, it's as small as a button now." Omed grinned down at her, so glad she was alive.

"I know you never kissed me because of my long nose," she whined under the effects of the anesthesia. "I wanted to be Aishwarya Rai. I told the surgeon to give me her nose and eyes. But it didn't work!" She clasped a palm over her nose in an effort to hide it.

"You're beautiful."

Her brow crinkled in protest. "No, you never cared. You idiot!" Then her eyes slowly closed, as she fell back to sleep. The nurse who stood by the bed put her hand to her mouth to suppress her laughter.

Omed scratched his head and walked out to the hospital yard for another smoke. He came back and sat on the half-broken bench in the ward corridor. Apparently, he had many thoughts he still needed to untangle. As the night passed and the corridor became less crowded, Omed's head fell to his shoulder, and he too surrendered to sleep.

* * *

The next morning Omed woke to the sound of Dushka fire and mortar shelling that rocked the city. Paying it no mind, he walked to the intensive care unit where Soz lay covered by a flowery blanket to the top of her head. When Omed tugged down the edge of the blanket, her eyes popped open. A faint smile drew her face upward when Omed placed a tiny kiss on the tip of her nose.

She cast down her eyes. "I hope I didn't say anything stupid while I was out of it."

"No, you were silent as a lamb."

She tilted her head to the side and looked around. "Where're my fatigues and my other gear?"

Omed plastered on his best poker face. "Rezan was here yesterday and picked up all your belongings from the nurse." He would make it right later. For now, Soz needed to concentrate on healing.

After a few moments, the nurse burst into the room and told Omed that the doctor needed to see him.

Omed's heart pounded in his chest as he walked to the doctor's office. He stood for a moment at the door, took a deep breath, and prepared himself to hear the worst. Then he stepped inside.

"Are you a family relation to Ms. Soz?" the doctor asked.

Omed wasn't prepared for that question. "No, I'm her friend. She's lost all her family."

The doctor leaned back in his chair. "A high-velocity bullet grazed her womb and caused other internal injuries; if she survives, she will be barren."

Omed nodded, but a frown marred his face as he remembered her words: *at least a half dozen of them to fill our future home.*

"Her condition remains critical, but there's something else I must talk with you about." The doctor opened a file on his desk. "It's about you."

"Me?" Omed asked, again filling with dread.

"You donated a unit of blood to the hospital yesterday?"

"Yes." He should have known his blood was too tainted to help anyone.

"There is an oddity in your blood."

Perhaps he could marry Soz before they both died here. "What is it, doctor? None of my life scenarios include dying on a bed."

"I am afraid you might. Your battle front has to change."

Omed laced his trembling fingers on his lap. "I'm ready to hear it."

"You have a rare enzyme in your blood. It's likely you have a rare antibody called Rh D immunoglobulin, or anti-D. If this is true, it could change your life and the lives of many others. You may have an antibody in your plasma that prevents Rhesus disease, a common and often fatal form of severe anemia in prenatal and neonatal infants."

Omed thought for a moment, every hair standing up on his body. "You mean I have lifesaving blood?"

"Can we contact the other members of your family? They might carry the same antibody."

"Perhaps they might carry it, but they can only help the people in Heaven. I'm the last apple on the tree."

"Aha." The doctor nodded as he made a note. "First we need to send a sample of your blood to Switzerland through the local Red Cross team. They'll do the testing to make the final determination."

A new, determined fire ignited inside Omed, as he asked, "What do I have to do?"

The doctor grinned. "Keep yourself alive. That antibody would make your blood so very precious to so many families and the babies they won't bury because of you."

As Omed walked out of the room, he slipped his hand under his collar and felt the scars on his chest. He thought about all the blood that had dripped from his body. It could've saved the life of a baby instead.

* * *

A few days later, the doctor talked with Soz while Omed waited in the hall. Her throat tightened, and unshed tears of fury, pain, and sorrow threatened to overflow from her eyes. Dark shadows lurked in the back of her mind as the doctor left the room.

Even so, as she saw Omed come through the door, a wry smile worked at her lips, and a sudden wave of warmth washed over her. She felt peace and tranquility in her soul. Her imagination danced and swam in purple clouds before she dared tiptoe into reality again.

"Here comes the hero," she teased.

"They say I have to stop fighting ISIS."

"More things than just riding in tanks can make you a hero. We are fighting on behalf of the world. There are many people on our side. You were born to do something else."

"I guess you'll have to let me go, one less worry for your team."

"I won't let you go that easily," Soz admitted, her voice thick with emotion. She shook her head gently to clear the haze of her desires, then teased, "The doctor said you're one of about forty people in the world who carries that rare blood in your veins."

As Omed nodded, Ashti entered the room. "How is the lady doing today?"

"Licking my wounds." Soz turned her gaze to Omed.

"She needed blood. Where have you been, man?" asked Omed.

"I hope she didn't receive your blood Omed; one psycho down here is enough!" He thought for a moment. "A rescue mission, retrieved a Yazidi girl from Raqqa."

Soz tried to rise from her bed, but Omed held her back. "What was her name, from which village?" she asked.

"Nazo," Ashti replied.

Soz's face clenched. "Not Soleen."

Omed's face lit up like a bulb. He fought to keep his shaking legs steady on the plastic chair. He bounded from his seat and asked Ashti to go outside with him for a smoke. She must never know how he burned with the desire to go to Nazo.

As they headed to the door, Soz called, "Omed, could you please visit this girl and ask her if she knows anything about my sister, Soleen?"

When Omed and Ashti entered the small lobby of the orphanage, Nazo was busy teaching the kids her special sign language to communicate with Sarah. As she turned to face him, Omed fought a tremendous urge to throw his arms around Nazo and never let her go.

Ashti said, "This is Omed, a fellow Yazidi from the Shingal region."

Nazo gazed at Omed's face as she stretched her arm for a handshake. "Haven't we met before?"

Omed's eyes caught on Nazo's bloated belly. "Yeah, though it seems like another life." He thought for a moment. "I did enjoy your melon, though." He mustered his best smile.

"Oh, you're the melon guy!" Nazo laughed.

Ashti joked, "Omed, I didn't know you sold melons!"

Omed remembered Soz's sister. "Have you met any girl named Soleen from Khanasor village during your travels?"

Nazo's face paled as the name gashed open an old wound. "Did you know her?"

"She's the sister of one of my friends here in Kobani."

"A woman named Soz?"

Omed nodded, pleased that Soz might find the answers she sought.

"She's here?"

"Yes, wounded in the hospital."

"I need to visit her."

The next afternoon, Omed sat beside Soz on her bed, holding her hand and talking, when Ashti and Nazo entered the room.

Omed rose to greet Nazo, who came forward, knelt to kiss Soz on both checks, then sat in a chair opposite Omed, who swallowed hard when Soz noticed his stolen glance at the beautiful girl.

Nazo turned to Soz. "I hope your wounds will heal soon."

Soz's eyes glittered as she turned her gaze from Omed to Nazo. "You mean my physical wounds?"

"Yeah, I know the others will never heal."

"I have a missing sister, Soleen; Omed said you might know something about her?"

"We were together." Nazo released a deep sigh.

"Oh, God." Soz swallowed her breath. "Where is she now?"

All the people in the room froze in apprehension of Nazo' next words. She took Soz's hands in hers. "She is in Heaven."

Soz's eyes rolled, and her body went lax as she fainted on the bed. Omed ran out to call for the doctor.

* * *

A few weeks later, Rezan brought Soz a new YBS uniform and helped her to dress in preparation to leave the hospital.

"Is Omed waiting for us outside?"

"No, Ashti will give us a ride." She paused, looking concerned. "Omed is at the orphanage."

Soz felt a sudden pang in her womb. "Let's pass by the orphanage. I need to talk to this girl."

Nazo and Omed were talking when the two women arrived at the orphanage lobby. Omed stood and walked toward Soz. He raised his eyebrows when he saw Soz in full combat gear with her AK-47 swung over her shoulder. "Oh, my commander is back on her feet!"

Soz looked at Nazo, then turned to Omed, struggling to keep the accusation from her voice. "I'm not sure you're under my command anymore."

Omed swept his eyes away to avoid looking in her face.

Ignoring the pang under her ribs, Soz turned to Nazo. "Tell me, how did she die?"

Nazo shook her head. "Why don't you try to remember how she lived?"

"Was she in great pain?"

Nazo thought for a moment. "I don't think she felt anything at the time. She kept calling your name till her face froze with a smile."

Soz's eyes turned dry, and she signaled to Rezan that she was ready to flee this nightmare.

As they turned to leave, Omed said, "Soz, I'm taking Nazo and Sarah across the border, all the way back to Iraqi Kurdistan. Why don't you join us back at our homes?"

Soz snorted. "We can't have homes until we drive this evil out of our lands or die trying."

Omed kept calling for Soz to wait, following them outside to insist. Instead, she and Rezan got into the waiting Humvee, and soon the two women disappeared behind the debris of destroyed buildings.

After a long, treacherous journey via Turkey, Omed, Nazo, and Sarah crossed the border to Iraqi Kurdistan. They arrived at the Internally Displaced Persons camp in the small town of Khanki that overlooked the Kurdish side of Mosul Lake. A shiver went through Nazo's body and memories fell in her mind like a drizzling rain. Khanki had been Azad's hometown.

Hundreds of white tents stretched across the lush hillsides carpeted in red wildflowers. The Yazidis' New Year feast, the *Charshamba Sur,* which fell on the second Wednesday of April, commemorated the time when Ta'us Malik calmed the Earth's quaking and spread his peacock colors throughout the world. Yet there were no signs of any celebration. The Yazidis instead mourned their dead and those who had been taken. Nevertheless, one of the boys who played hopscotch outside the camp gave Nazo a colored egg, a symbol of fertility in the New Year.

The two women were happy to be among their people again. As they walked to their tent in sector 4, a few women stared at her bloated belly and whispered to each other with deep frowns, certain she had converted to another religion and carried a baby from their most hated enemy.

A week later, a Kurdish interpreter asked if a German aid worker named Angelika could hear Nazo and Sarah's story. Upon entering their tent, the German lady noted Nazo's large belly. As Nazo told of their trials, the woman's eyes grew moist as well. She asked for all of Nazo and Sarah's details and then asked them to visit the passport office in Dohuk to obtain new passports. She told Nazo through the interpreter that she would do her best to help them to receive permanent residency and education, as well as medical and psychological help under an initiative for traumatized Yazidi girls and women introduced by the German state of Baden-Wurttemberg. Nazo burst into fresh tears as she realized she was about to fulfill Azad's long-awaited dream.

That afternoon, as she had yearned to do for so long, Nazo finally stepped in bare feet into the Holy Lalish Temple. The large, mystical snake-image on the smooth, tan stone to the right of the doorway greeted her. She kissed the pillar and carefully stepped over the threshold.

Once inside, she lit four candles and prayed for the souls of Azad and her family. She doused herself four times in the holy waters of the Zam Zam, the spring beneath the temple. Then, as she approached the tomb of Sheikh Adi, she knotted her silk ribbon and made her wish to the Supreme God to forgive her sins and bless her with a blue-eyed baby.

When the evening came, a group of pilgrims packed the temple's courtyard, burning cotton wicks in their hands. Baba Sheikh, the Yazidi spiritual leader, and other religious men emerged from the entrance barefoot and stepped over the threshold. Baba Sheikh's bearded face glowed in the light of the burning cotton wick as Nazo approached him to pay her respects and seek his advice.

Clad in his white cloak, he sat cross-legged. "Daughter, we know you were forced to convert, and you have my respect," said the Sheikh.

"Baba Sheikh, what shall I do about their remarks that I carry one of our enemies?" asked Nazo as she knelt to kiss his hand.

Baba Sheikh tapped Nazo's shoulder. "Be brave and strong, my daughter."

That evening, Baba Sheikh issued a statement encouraging Yazidis to accept the women returning from ISIS and to help reintegrate these victims, as they had been "subjected to matters outside their control." This statement eased much of the burden on Nazo and the other women and girls who had escaped their enemies.

* * *

One early morning, a local aid worker approached Nazo and asked if her pregnancy were increasing her burden, making it harder for her to cope with what had happened to her. "Though abortion is illegal in this region unless a doctor decides that giving birth to the child will threaten the life of the mother, I could offer you abortion pills, but it's too late, I guess. Most pregnant girls who return from ISIS slavery either take the pills or carry out an abortion themselves," said the, woman.

Nazo shook her head. "But I wish to keep my baby."

The woman's eyebrows rose in surprise, but she didn't press the issue further.

Near midnight several days later, Nazo awoke to the clap of thunder announcing a spring rainstorm. The wind made the tent walls flap like the beat of a drumroll. The rain hissed down and leaked into the tent to drench the thin foam mattress under her. She moaned in pain as her stomach cramped and twisted. She rose, put a towel on her head, and walked into the rain, headed for the makeshift camp clinic.

One of the women from a neighboring tent grabbed Nazo's arm to steady her while Nazo concentrated on walking. The thick layers of mud that caked their plastic shoes slowed their walk, and afraid she would slip and fall, Nazo paused to remove them. Then they continued, holding their mud-caked shoes in their hands. They were both muddy to their knees and soaked through with rain by the time they arrived at the clinic in the middle of the camp.

As Nazo lay on the delivery table in the medical tent, an old midwife scurried in and out, fetching warm water and clean, dry linens. The tent's battery was losing its charge, and the lights dimmed as Nazo's agonized and terrified screams grew louder.

Then she felt Azad's hand touch her forehead. Confident, no longer afraid, she stomped the table rhythmically, swinging her hips, grunting and groaning in an expression of strength during her contractions.

Soon she let out a primal scream.

The midwife smiled as she rose, lifting the wailing newborn into the air. She wrapped the boy in a small blanket and gave him to Nazo. Even as she soared, elated to hold her baby for the first time, she burned with the desire to see his eyes. Nazo fixed her gaze on his face, and a few moments later, blazing dark-blue eyes peered from the blanket while a smirk curled his lips.

With a triumphant wail of heartbreaking joy, Nazo released the mountain of despair that had dwelled in the depths of her soul for the last nine months.

The next morning, while Nazo sat in her tent and breastfed her baby and Sarah gazed over her shoulder at the newcomer, the flap of the tent was yanked open. An old man accompanied by a mob of angry men who had lost members of their families to ISIS rushed in. Someone grabbed her. As she wailed, the old man yanked the baby from her and hurried toward the lake while other men held her firmly by the arms.

Nazo broke free from their grasp and ran as fast as she could after the others. As she drew closer, the men shoved her back until she fell to the ground, crying, "Daesh don't have blue eyes! Daesh don't have blue eyes! My baby has blue eyes!" She fought to regain her footing and ran to the boat but was ensnared by the strength of two men.

While she struggled, Omed arrived panting and ran toward the boat before the men could shove off for the middle of the lake, where they would plunge her boy into the water.

At the dock, one of the men had unfastened the rope from the ring, and another was firing up the small outboard motor, while the old man sat in the middle of the boat after tossing her boy between his feet.

Omed leaped onboard. "You crazy old coot! You're going to kill your own grandson! This is Azad's child!"

The old man's face froze, then he leaned and tilted his head down. His old blue eyes couldn't have been more than a few inches away from her baby's face. Nazo breathed a sigh of relief when the man untied her baby's white headdress and caressed his pale blond hair with a rough hand.

Omed kneeled down beside the old man. "See, blond hair and blue eyes. The baby carries the Yazidis' ancient Aryan bloodline."

The old man held the baby in his arms and walked toward Nazo, followed by Omed and other men. He leaned forward and placed the baby in her arms again.

She closed her eyes to the tears that followed as she clutched her son tight to her heaving chest. The old man helped Nazo to her feet and walked away.

* * *

The next day, while Nazo sat at the tent door with her baby on her lap and enjoyed the sun warming her body, the old man, Hassan Seydo, approached her. She instinctively tightened her grip on her baby.

"How is my great grandson doing this morning?" He leaned over the baby, as if again checking for the tiny blue eyes.

"He's good at keeping me and the people in the neighboring tents awake all night." Nazo smiled, hoping it looked natural and relaxed.

"I want to teach him to be a fisherman. That would make him calm and patient."

"Maybe you should teach him to swim first, so he won't drown the next time someone decides to throw him into the lake!"

The old man's face wrinkled in chagrin. "Let's take a walk to the lake then."

"Isn't it a bit early for swimming lessons?"

"Yes, but it's time for him to meet his father."

A speck of fear pierced Nazo's heart.

Before she could find her voice, Hassan Seydo continued, "A few weeks ago, the Peshmerga forces liberated your village from the Daesh, and we were able to retrieve Azad's body from a mass grave near the village." He released a deep sigh. "We reburied him at our local cemetery on the banks of the lake."

Nazo's eyes moistened, as she grabbed the baby's white bundle and rose to follow the old man.

When they arrived at the small hillside that overlooked the lake, Nazo placed the baby on the ground and crouched to pick a handful of the red flowers.

Hassan Seydo guided her to Azad's grave. She sat by his gravestone and placed his son on his grave. Then she rose and seized the bunch of the red flowers in her hand. Leaf from leaf, she tore them. They fell from her hand one by one along with her falling tears.

* * *

Two months later, Nazo waited in the lobby of the Erbil International Airport with her baby in her lap, surrounded by Angelika, Omed, and Sarah.

When the loudspeaker announced for the passengers of the Erbil-Stuttgart flight to board the plane, Angelika rose and signaled for the women to follow her.

Nazo stood and turned to Omed. "Time to go. If it weren't forbidden, I'd give you a big hug right now."

Omed came forward and hugged Nazo so hard that the baby was squeezed between them and began to cry.

"You're psycho, you know." She laughed with tears in her eyes.

As a last farewell, Omed placed a tiny kiss on her baby's forehead. "Azad was a lucky man."

Baby Azad giggled as they left Omed, who stood waving goodbye.

Nazo walked with slow but confident steps behind Angelika and Sarah down the corridor, then the aisle of the plane. She found her seat and sat her baby in her lap. She was no longer scared of what the future had in store for her. Yet when she closed her eyes, dark memories rained down on her. When the plane rose into the sky, little Azad wailed as his ears popped.

* * *

Omed walked out of the airport and headed across the street, looking down in deep thought. A speeding red car zoomed toward him. The woman honked her horn jarringly and swerved to avoid him. The car screeched to a halt, narrowly missing him.

The woman leaned out the window and yelled, "Hey, watch where you're going, you idiot!"

Hearing this, Omed remembered Soz's letter. He smiled and yelled back, "Yes, I am a total idiot! I was blind, and I couldn't see where I was going. Thank you—you saved my life!"

Omed continued his walk with purpose, now heading to the taxi stop.

"Where to, sir?" asked the driver.

"The bus terminal to Turkey."

By the next morning, Omed walked the streets of Gazi-Antap. He did some shopping before he headed to the Syrian-Turkish border to sneak into Kobani.

That afternoon he arrived at the border inn and contacted Ashti to arrange for his crossing. He climbed a hilltop that over-looked Kobani from the Turkish side of the border. He took off his backpack and crouched beside a group of elderly Kurdish men who had come to watch the ongoing battle. A short distance away, he could see Turkish soldiers and tanks waiting all along the border. While the elderly men conversed about the fate of the rest of their families still trapped in Kobani, Omed stared at his cell phone. An hour later, the phone rang, and he received the instructions for his crossing. Ashti awaited him at the specified point, and in the dark of the night, both entered Kobani from the northeastern portion of the border.

* * *

Early in the morning, Rezan sat on the floor of her tent, twisting Soz's hair into an elaborate braid that started from the top of her head. Other fighters were doing their final weapons and ammunition inspections before going out on a mission.

"Look who's here!" Rezan turned with her hands still in Soz's hair.

Soz stared at the reflection of Omed's face in the shard of broken mirror in her hand. All came forward to greet Omed, the missing member of their team, except Soz, who sat and watched through the mirror.

The idiot headed to his locker to pick up his military outfit and his fighting gear.

Soz stood and turned to Omed. "What are you doing?"

"What I'm supposed to be doing: fighting with my team."

"You know you can't do that. I won't allow it."

"I was hoping you'd let me join anyway."

"You know it would be a big problem if you were seriously wounded."

Omed donned his ammunition vest and swung his AK-47 on his left shoulder. "You have your last bullet in your pocket, so shoot me then." He broke into a smile.

Soz picked up her gun from the corner of the room and stalked out, and Omed and the rest of the team followed her.

The mission was a raid on an abandoned village southwest of Kobani. A group of ISIS fighters had snuck into the village earlier to stage suicide attacks. Soz's unit arrived in the aftermath of an apparent airstrike that targeted expected ISIS hideouts in the village with two large blasts. A huge plume of smoke and flames rose over the northern part of the village. As the team advanced toward a bombed-out building from two sides, a hail of gunfire came at them from an adjacent mud-brick house. Soz and her comrades took positions about fifty yards from the house's main gate.

Over the chanting of the YBS fighters as they charged toward the house with their weapons ready, someone inside called, "We'll enslave and behead all of you worthless creatures!"

Rezan unleashed a burst of gunfire through the iron gate. "Come out, old rat! Come out if you're a real man!" she yelled.

"We'll drive you out from here into Hell!"

Soz replied, "We Yazidi Kurds have lived here for five thousand years! No one can drive us out!"

Soz and Omed snaked through the crossfire until they were in range to throw their hand grenades into the house's inner yard. They each took a grenade from their ammunition vests, then looked at each other. On Soz's third head nod, their two grenades flew over the wall into the yard.

After the two successive blasts, the whole team rushed into the house. None of the four ISIS fighters survived the grenade attack.

As the team members scrambled to secure the house while removing ammunition vests and assault rifles from the dead bodies, Omed approached Soz. With the pin ring from his thrown grenade in his hand, he knelt down at her feet. "Having you by my side will complete me. Soz, I wish I could give you everything, but I hope this ring will prove that I would die for you."

Soz burst to tears as she stretched her hand. "Yes! Yes! A thousand times, yes!" She threw her arms around his neck and hugged him tightly.

The smell of burned gunpowder clogged his nose as he slipped the oversized pin ring on her muddy finger. All the team members gathered around them and clapped with enthusiasm.

Rezan, with unshed tears in her eyes, came forward and hugged them both.

A few days later, Soz received a letter from the YBS regional commander stating that her team's mission in Kobani was now complete. The whole town had been liberated from ISIS. The team was to relocate to its original base in the Shingal region.

PESHMERGA FORCES liberated Omed's village, but the surviving villagers were reluctant to return while ISIS fighters still patrolled in the area, taking aid and comfort from the nearby Arab farmhouses. Despite this, Soz and Omed returned to his village to celebrate their wedding. Omed had invited all the members of their team and the Peshmerga from the neighboring bunkers to attend. Of course, Soz remained vigilant. She peered through the binoculars at the Arab village below and then turned to Omed. "I need to coordinate with the Peshmerga commander. We have to drive the people from the Arab village and force them south to a safer distance."

"They were our neighbors. We coexisted in peace for centuries." Said Omed.

"You cannot coexist with people who want to pull the rug out from under your feet. Have you forgotten how our neighbors turned against us and sided with the Daesh when they killed our men and took our women as slaves?"

"I remember. It was crazy. We've attended each other's weddings and funerals. We've slept at each other's homes, eaten from the same plate, drank from the same teapot. Then next day, they mounted black flags on their houses and vehicles. Clad in black, they covered their faces and raided our villages. Suddenly, we brothers of yesterday became the infidels. They think it is the will of God."

Omed reached to stroke her cheek. "Then we leave the matter to God—if a goat eats the shepherd's dinner, that does not mean the shepherd has to slaughter the goat."

Soz leaned into his touch. "True, but the shepherd has to hit the goat with his cane, so it won't happen again."

Omed snaked his hands around her neck. "Come on. You're overthinking this. Let's discuss the wedding arrangements."

* * *

The bride's unit awaited her inside an abandoned house. Soz removed the two wedding pillows she'd embroidered from the rear seat of the Humvee. Rezan followed her into the house carrying the wedding gown and helped Soz slip into her dress. Then Rezan fastened the huge, embossed silver buckle around her slender waist. The female members of the team had made a necklace from pink oleander blossoms and slipped it around Soz's neck as a charm against the Evil Eye.

The procession started from the abandoned house toward Omed's house, with the bride walking ahead of the group of the female fighters dancing to the rhythm of the *dahol* drum and *zorna* flute.

When the procession reached the bridegroom's home, Omed stood on the roof near the entrance and threw a jar full of rice, sweets, and money notes down in front of the bride. The male and female fighters laughed, pushing each other away like kids, and knelt down to collect the sweets and money notes from the ground. Then Omed threw an apple at the bride's head when she raised her eyes to get a look at her groom. This would ensure her future obedience, so she wouldn't repeat Eve's mistake with Adam.

Rezan walked around with a henna dish. Women and girls dipped their fingers into the henna and put money into the dish as a wedding gift. The sound of the *dahul* and the *zorna* filled the air around Soz. The Peshmerga and Yazidi YBS fighters formed their own traditional dance circles. When Soz took Omed's hand and joined the dance, the music grew louder and more zealous. The two dance circles merged, forming one big Kurdish circle.

That night Rezan acted as the bride's mentor. She whispered naughty suggestions in Soz's ear as she slipped a small piece of white cloth into Soz's hand. Then the bride and groom walked into their bedroom.

A few minutes later, Soz jumped when the door flew open from a well-timed kick. The men from Soz's team burst in, teasing the couple and making a ruckus. Soz giggled as Rezan swooped in behind them with a broomstick in her hands and ran after the fleeing men. Then she closed the door to fend off further raids.

A little later, Soz knocked on the door from inside and slipped the small piece of white cloth, smeared with a few drops of blood, under the door. A cheer soon went up from all her team members in the front yard, where she assumed they were planning their next prank. A few rounds were fired into the air to announce the conquest. The music picked up as Soz peered out the window, hoping to catch a glimpse as her team formed a dance circle, whirling to the rhythm of folk songs they began to sing.

* * *

On a bright morning in late autumn, Omed and Soz walked hand-in-hand outside the village. The crisp air slowed their steps. The fresh scent of a rainstorm wafted from the drops on the brilliant, fallen leaves. A colossal flock of birds traveled across the handful of fluffy clouds floating in the clear sky. Omed couldn't imagine a greater day. They arrived at the fig tree by the well. The sound of the breeze caressing the leaves filled his ears. Soz ran giggling for the swing. She sat and pumped her feet back and forth.

Omed stood behind her and gave her a gentle push. A yellow-brown leaf tumbled from the tree and landed on Omed's head. He brushed it away and guided the swing to a stop, then threw his arms around Soz and held her back tightly to his chest. As she turned her head, Omed placed a kiss on her nose. She broke free from him and ran toward the well, teasing and laughing.

He ran toward her and grabbed her around the waist. A low brick wall encircled the well. They both tumbled down next to the wall and rolled in the mud. Omed rose from the muddy ground panting. He helped Soz to her feet and slapped off the wet leaves that clung to her dress. Then they sat down together on the low wall.

Omed knelt down and picked up a tiny leaf from the ground. He placed the leaf on Soz's lips and asked her to close her eyes. He pressed his lips to the other side of the leaf. He felt a shiver run through Soz's body as he slowly swept the leaf away and kissed her closed lips.

* * *

Almost too far away for the lovebirds to see, two ISIS fighters crouched on the roof of an abandoned house in the southern part of the village.

Nashwan, the Arab boy from Soz's high school, watched Omed and Soz through his binoculars as the couple sat kissing on the well wall.

The sniper eased the barrel of his rifle through a hole in the low concrete wall of the house. Then he whispered to Nashwan that he had a clear shot.

Nashwan took his left hand from his binoculars and felt the scar on his chest from Soz's mattock. "Take the man."

The sniper pulled the trigger. The shot echoed across the village. A cluster of black crows that nestled in the fig tree flew away, sending more leaves tumbling around the lovers.

Omed's head jerked. Blood splashed Soz's face. He fell down on his side next to the well. Soz screamed as his blood streamed into the colorful tumbled leaves.

* * *

After four weeks of inconsolable mourning, Soz sat on the bathroom floor and slid the razor over her skin. She drew an X where her heart used to be. Her stark, red blood stood out against her skin. Her tears flowed freely, dripping off her cheek and mingling with the blood that dribbled down her breast.

As she watched the trails of red drops running down her chest, the pain allowed her, for a few moments, to forget the shattering image of Omed's last breath, forget how his rivulets of ebbing life had washed the tiny raindrops from the leaves. Indeed, the pain over her heart lessened the pain inside it, just as Omed had said it would.

When she thought of him, she let out a piercing wail, a plea for help, for release from her misery and rage, followed by the maniacal laughter of one long past help and ecstatic in her madness.

Following his ritual, she took her fingertip and dipped it into her flowing blood. Then she rinsed the droplets away and cleansed her cuts with Omed's flammable antiseptic.

Shaking, unsure that this would bring her the relief she so desperately sought, she took out her lighter and set fire to the letter she had written to Omed in Kobani. The burning paper released acrid smoke, as she brought the flames closer. They made contact with her skin and singed the huge X over her heart. The sting was intense, but she felt relief. Yes, Omed, it did release so much of her anger and anguish.

She left the bathroom and slipped into her YBS outfit. As she picked up her AK-47 from the corner of the hall, Rezan rushed in panting.

"We got him."

"Alive?"

Rezan nodded.

Soz's heart beat double time as they both rushed out. The familiar face of Nashwan greeted her from the trunk of the truck. With his hands tied behind his back, he was at her mercy.

Too bad he'd murdered her only reason to be merciful. Soz yanked him out of the truck to the ground. She knelt down and looked him in the eyes. "Now you'll be killed by a woman. What an end!"

"By two women." Rezan aimed her rifle at his head. Soz stretched her hand into his shirt and felt the uneven scar on his chest from her small mattock. Then she walked back to the yard of the house and brought two big mattocks. She gave one to Rezan. Spending their rage, they dug deep into his flesh. Blood spurted on their hands and bodies with each swing. Once they were satisfied, they walked to the cemetery and stood by Omed's gravestone. Soz pulled out her bayonet and asked Rezan to help her cut her braid. Then, fighting fresh tears, she knelt down and hung her braid on his gravestone. They both wept for their lost loves and their lost innocence. For the next week, Soz felt sick. For a while, she thought it might be from brutally taking a man's life, but Rezan escorted her to a small hospital in one of the neighboring towns. The doctor examined her and requested a urine test. Half an hour later, the test results arrived.

"Congratulations, you're pregnant," said the doctor.

"Oh, my God!" Soz smiled for the first time in weeks.

Then her head spun and her eyes rolled. Rezan grabbed her right arm before she hit the ground. They laid her half-conscious on the examination table.

When she roused from her faint, she cried, "My tubes are damaged. I'm unable to conceive children."

The doctor shook his head. "The results are certain."

Rezan hugged her tight. "It seems you'll bring another Yazidi into this world."

Epilogue

As the ancient Yazidi prophecy stated, the Golden Age had commenced. The Yazidis emigrated to the four corners of the Earth. Their spiritual message prevailed, delivered to the representatives of all nations.

Soz watched the colorful falling leaves of wild vines drift past her window. A soft chill caressed her face as she turned her gaze to the people outside, basking in the haze of the early autumn sun in the German town of Oberwesel.

She put the final layer on the cake she'd prepared for young Omed's seventeenth birthday. On the TV, the news anchor announced that the president of the Kurdistan Republic would visit Germany next week to join their efforts to combat terrorism.

The doorbell rang. Nazo and young Azad appeared at the door. Everyone gathered at the kitchen table laden with Kurdish food.

"Sarah asked me to convey her best wishes for you, Omed." Nazo turned to Soz. "You know she thinks the whole stock market will collapse if she leaves her money exchange for one moment."

Azad pulled out a dining room chair, but before he could sit, Omed yanked it away.

From the floor, Azad shouted, "You're a psycho, you know that?"

Everyone laughed except Soz who had traveled back in time, thinking of young Omed's father, her charming psycho. She could still feel the taste of their last kiss on her lips.

Even after Omed blew out the seventeen candles on his cake, the memories in Soz's mind remained in flames. The two mothers picked at the figs from the fruit tray on the table. Nazo's eyes glistened with tears as well, and a tremendous urge surfaced in Soz to revisit the memories buried in the depth of their gray souls.

Nazo picked up her *daf* from the leather bag and played. All gathered around her and sang in Kurdish. Along with the rattling of the *daf* chains, through the half-open window, a wolf howled from the neighboring forest. A distant smile crept to the corner of Nazo's mouth as she continued playing her tunes.

A while later, Nazo put down the frame drum and released a sigh. The two ladies gazed at each other for a moment.

"It's time," Soz announced.

* * *

When the four arrived at the Red Cross Donation Center in Mainz, the receptionist asked Omed if he spoke German and gave him a form to fill out. In their near perfect German, Omed and Azad discussed his weird, healing blood for a moment and then Azad asked if he could donate too.

Five minutes later, they both lay on donation tables. They made faces at each other and snickered as the young, blond German nurse approached. "Are you ready?" she asked.

Azad fixed her with his blue eyes. "I'm ready to sacrifice my blood for you to the very last drop."

"Knock off with that, and let's pump some Yazidi blood into the new citizens of the world." Omed laughed, thrilled to fulfill the promise that his father never could.